PENGUIN BOOKS

U   w̄1ı

Unknown

DIDIER VAN CAUWELAERT

Translated from the French by
Mark Polizzotti

PENGUIN BOOKS

PENGUIN BOOKS

Published by the Penguin Group
Penguin Books Ltd, 80 Strand, London WC2R ORL, England
Penguin Group (USA) Inc., 375 Hudson Street, New York, New York 10014, USA
Penguin Group (Canada), 90 Eglinton Avenue East, Suite 700, Toronto, Ontario,
Canada M4P 2Y3 (a division of Pearson Penguin Canada Inc.)
Penguin Ireland, 25 St Stephen's Green, Dublin 2, Ireland
(a division of Penguin Books Ltd)
Penguin Group (Australia), 250 Camberwell Road, Camberwell,
Victoria 3124, Australia (a division of Pearson Australia Group Pty Ltd)
Penguin Books India Pvt Ltd, 11 Community Centre,
Panchsheel Park, New Delhi – 110 017, India
Penguin Group (NZ), 67 Apollo Drive, Rosedale, Auckland 0632,
New Zealand (a division of Pearson New Zealand Ltd)
Penguin Books (South Africa) (Pty) Ltd, 24 Sturdee Avenue,
Rosebank, Johannesburg 2196, South Africa

Penguin Books Ltd, Registered Offices: 80 Strand, London WC2R ORL, England

www.penguin.com

First published in French as *Hors de moi* by Éditions Albin Michel S.A. 2003
This translation first published in the USA as
Out of My Head by Other Press LLC, New York 2004
Published in Penguin Books 2011

1

Copyright © Éditions Albin Michel S.A., 2003
Translation copyright © Mark Polizzotti, 2004
All rights reserved

The moral right of the author has been asserted

Set in 13.5/16 pt Garamond MT
Typeset by Ellipsis Books Limited, Glasgow
Printed in England by Clays Ltd, St Ives plc

978-0-241-95123-1

www.greenpenguin.co.uk

I

I've just rung at my apartment and a strange man answered. Taken aback, I stare at the intercom.

'Yes,' the voice repeats.

'Sorry, my mistake.'

The crackling stops. The buttons are very close together; I must have pressed the neighbor's instead. With my finger centered squarely on my name, I press the little black rectangle once more.

'Now what?' says the same voice, impatiently.

Probably a crossed wire. Or a workman who's there to finish the remodeling.

'Is this the fourth floor, left?'

'Yes.'

'Is my wife there?'

'Who?'

I'm about to tell him that I'm Martin Harris, but the building door opens and a couple with twin cell phones spills out, listening to their messages. I walk across the foyer and straight into the wooden elevator, which shudders slowly up to the top floor.

The landing is dark. I feel around for the timer switch, then press my doorbell. The neighbor's door opens after a moment and a little old man passes one eye over the chain. I say hello. He answers, in a tone that's at once guilty and suspicious, that all the doorbells sound the same. I agree, explain that I don't have my keys, turn around as my door opens. A man wearing pajamas, backlit, gives me the once-over. The words stick in my throat.

'Are you the one who keeps ringing the intercom?'

I ask what he's doing there.

'What do you mean, what am *I* doing here?'

'In my house.'

'*Your* house?'

The sincerity of his astonishment leaves me nonplussed. As I begin making out the features of his face, I explain with forced calm that I am Mr Harris. He jumps. Thoughts begin to crowd into my head, of the most pathetic and insecure kind. My wife is seeing another man, she moved him in here while I was in the hospital.

'Liz!'

We've both called out at the same time. She appears at the door to the bathroom, in panties and a black blouse. I start making my way into the apartment, but he blocks my way. She asks what's going on. She asks *him* what's going on.

'Nothing,' he says. 'An error.'

She looks at me. Not like a cheating wife caught red-handed but like a stranger you accost who turns away, wanting no part of you.

'You deal with it,' she says to him.

And she disappears into the kitchen. I take a step, but the other man grabs me by the arm. I shout, 'Liz! What's gotten into you!'

'You leave my wife alone!'

His wife? I stand there with my mouth hanging open, my momentum broken by his aplomb. He is more or less my age, thinner, with a better-pitched voice, a square-shaped head, disheveled blond hair, and he's wearing the Hermès pajamas that Liz bought me at Kennedy Airport. I knock his arm down with my fist.

'What the hell!' he shouts, pushing me back.

'Is there a problem, Mr Harris?'

I turn around. The neighbor is still behind his door chain.

'No, everything's fine, Mr Renaudat,' the other man answers. 'It's all under control.'

I gape at each of them, incredulous.

'Are you sure?' the neighbor insists.

'Yes, yes. It's just a misunderstanding. I'm sorry I woke you up. We're not going to get the whole building involved, are we?' he segues in a lower voice, staring at me as if trying to reason me into some kind of reconciliation. 'Come on, come inside so we can talk this over . . .'

I grab him by my pajamas, yank him out onto the landing.

'No, *you* get out of my house, and I mean now! We'll talk this over in front of witnesses!'

'Martin!' my wife cries out.

He frees himself with a backhanded slap. In the time it takes me to react, my door has slammed in my face. I spin toward the little old man, who jumps back, slams his own door shut, and gives the deadbolt two full turns. Swallowing back my stupor, I try to find the natural tone of voice one uses in such situations. 'Hello, Mr Renaudat, excuse me, I'm your new neighbor. I haven't had a chance to introduce myself yet.' He screams at me to go away or he'll call the police.

I remain frozen in the silence of the landing, with no explanation for this absurdity. How can you prove what's obvious when everyone denies it, and you've got no proof to offer other than your own good faith? I love my wife, she loves me, we've never fought in front of people, I've only cheated on her once in ten years of marriage and even then it was just professional, a colleague at a botanists' convention, she never knew about it, we were looking forward to our new life in Paris – what's the meaning of this? I come home and suddenly find myself in some kind of *Candid Camera* situation. I look around the landing for mics, a hidden lens, reflections behind the mirror . . . But who would have staged such a prank, and why would Liz play along?

The timer on the hallway light runs out. I lean against the wall to catch my breath. My throat feels tight, my head is spinning, and in the pit of my stomach is the mix of anxiety and relief you feel when a bad premonition finally comes true. Since waking up I've been trying in vain to reach my wife on her cell phone. I've been missing for a week and she wasn't even worried, didn't report my disappearance, didn't go to the police, who would have given her the name of the hospital where I was recovering. And now this morning, she's pretending to be married to someone else.

Immobile in the shadows of the landing, I stare at my door, hoping it will open and Liz will come out laughing, introduce her accomplice, and throw her arms around my neck with a shout of 'April fool!' But it's 30 October, and she's never been one for practical jokes. Nor for having a lover. Or so I thought. In the span of two minutes, I've found myself thrown out of my own home, not sure of anything anymore.

And then the situation suddenly becomes clear and I break into a smile, realizing how stupid the whole thing is. She thought I'd left her flat, that I'd just run away with the blonde in the window seat who'd been flirting with me above the Atlantic. I figured Liz hadn't noticed, what with her two sleeping pills and cloth mask . . . I thought she was acting strangely when we landed, but she always scowls at younger women. Leaving the airport, as I tried to cheer her up, she hissed under her breath, 'Very discreet of you!' And when I bent down to pick up the belt of her raincoat, she slammed the taxi door on my hand.

'Liz, listen to me, it's not what you think! I was in a car accident, I was in a coma for three days, it's all right now, there are no lasting effects, but the hospital wanted to keep me under observation . . . I've been trying to call you since I woke up, there's a problem with your cell . . . Listen to me, open up! What's going on here? I'm exhausted, my hand hurts, I need a shower, and . . . Liz! Open the door, goddammit!'

No answer. Utter silence in the apartment. Listen as I might, all I hear is the sound of the elevator behind me. I try to kick the door down.

'Cut it out! I'm in no shape for this! Open this door or I'll break it in! You hear me?'

A giant surges from the elevator and wraps his arms around me.

'Take it easy.'

'Let me go!'

'Everything's fine, Mr Renaudat, I've got him under control.'

The sound of a deadbolt from the neighbor's. His door opens again and the little old man yelps, 'What's the use of paying for an intercom and a super if you let just anybody come in?'

I shout that this is *my* building.

'I said take it easy!' the huge guy answers, crushing my ribs.

He thanks the neighbor for alerting him and asks me what I want with Mr Harris.

'But *I'm* Mr Harris!'

The vise of his biceps loosens, then immediately squeezes in again. With the tip of his chin, he rings my doorbell, then calls out, 'Sorry to bother you, Mr Harris, but is this person related to you?'

'Absolutely not!' answers the man behind the door. 'I've never laid eyes on him before.'

'Well?' the concierge barks at me as if this were proof I was lying.

'Well what? I've never seen him before either. I don't know him!'

'But I do. That's Mr Harris, he lives here, and I'm the building superintendent. Okay? So you get the hell out of here this minute or I'm calling the cops.'

I break free with a sharp jerk and grab him by his polo shirt.

'Go ahead! Call them! Do it now! This guy is an impostor pretending he's me and my wife is going along with it!'

Nothing stirs in his brutish face.

'Have you got any ID?'

I slip my hand into my jacket pocket out of

habit, then let it fall. I explain that I was in an accident and lost my wallet.

'Don't let him fool you!' cries the neighbor. 'He's just some junkie, you can see it on his face!'

I'm about to answer that I have the face of someone who just got out of hospital, but I change my mind. They'll take me for an escaped mental patient. I turn back toward my door, call out in a supplicating voice, 'Liz, I love you! Please, stop this charade . . . Tell them who I am!'

I speak in English. She's from Quebec and we always communicated in French, back in Greenwich; it gave us a sense of privacy that I try to recreate here on the landing, in reverse. I swear to her that she's the only one in my life. Still no reply. I catch a darting glance between the super and the neighbor. It can't be – is everyone in on it? But this glance is less about connivance than insinuation. Like the wink two misogynists give each other in front of a woman they've classed as a slut: she hooked up with a guy without telling him she was married and now he's raising a stink because he's jealous, so she's making like she doesn't know him from Adam.

'Come on, pal,' murmurs the concierge in a

gentler voice. 'You can see you're not welcome here.'

I look back at him for a moment, then nod, overwhelmed by the glint of humanity that passed through his bovine eyes. As if he identified with me, as if he empathized with the misunderstanding and rejection I've unleashed. His hand pats my shoulder in a gesture of solidarity for the kind of pathetic slob who invents a life for himself at the bar after work.

He prods me toward the elevator. I don't resist.

'And don't let me catch you hanging around the neighborhood, buddy. You got it?' he says in the lobby, with a real gentleness. 'Or I'll have to kick your ass. They don't like to be bothered around here.'

I can feel his eyes on my back as I walk toward the glass entrance door. When it has shut behind me, I turn around. Through my transparent reflection, I see him going back into his office.

'Look out!' shouts a kid on rollerblades, brushing past me.

The noises of the street fade in around me: a garbage truck, a jackhammer, passers-by, car horns. Everything's normal, everything's as before.

I look at myself in the glass doors and I'm the same. The same thick-set, rumpled outline, stiff hair, and unremarkable face. It wouldn't take much to convince myself that nothing had happened. I've just arrived at my building, I ring at the door, Liz opens it, and we rush into each other's arms. Where *were* you, I was going crazy with worry, what happened to you? Then I'll tell her about the accident, the coma, regaining consciousness, her cell phone not working; she'll make us some coffee and we'll head back to the hospital to settle my bill. The scene I've been playing over and over in my head since coming to. The one that was supposed to happen. My finger hesitates above my name on the black button. Then I turn and leave the street.

I walk like a robot among scurrying pedestrians and tourists, looking for a familiar face in spite of myself, a shopkeeper who might have seen me with Liz, any witness at all to hold onto. But there are only antiques dealers and clothing boutiques. I turn right, head to the drugstore they'd told me about last Thursday. I try to find the girl who bandaged my hand, describe her. She's on vacation. I leave, retrace my steps, walk by the window of the France Télécom outlet where Liz bought our cell phones. But they're prepaids and don't involve any particular interaction with the sales clerk – and in any case, she already had them by the time I came back from the drugstore to find her.

I go into the first café I see and collapse onto a seat. I don't feel good. My head is spinning, my thoughts are getting bogged down, and I'm so tired I can hardly stand. The medicine they gave me, the tetanus vaccine, the side effects of what I've been through ... I'm no longer myself. As if the fact of being denied like this, attacked in my very identity, were somehow contagious. 'You'll see,' the neurologist told me, 'some memories might have been erased, or will take time to come back.' But that's not it – everything is there, in its place. It's horrible not to feel any uncertainty and still be so short of convincing arguments. My memory is intact, but it's running on idle, without echo, with nothing to catch onto, dissociated.

With my elbows on the table and my head in my hands, I breathe in the smell of beer and cold ashtrays to get a grip on the present, chase away the vision that's haunting me. I felt like a stranger in the eyes of my own wife. And she looked sincere. Some painting contractors are laughing loudly at the bar, full of life, covered in stains and plaster bits. I quickly review the list of who I've spoken to since arriving on French soil, who could possibly confirm that I'm me. The cop at passport control, but I didn't really notice his face. The Korean taxi driver who brought us here, but I didn't keep the receipt. And then the woman who was in the accident with me, of course, but she doesn't know any more about me than what I told her, just like the staff at the hospital.

'What'll it be?'

I look at the waiter. No point asking if he recognizes me. We came to sit there for a moment with our luggage, unwrapping our new cell phones, while waiting for our appointment with the land-lord. Then I realized that I'd left my computer at the airport. Liz stayed behind to wait for the keys and I hopped into a cab. After that came the accident, the coma, my reawakening.

'Sir? What can I get you?' the waiter insists.

I hesitate. I don't know what I want. I don't know what I drink.

'Something strong.'

'A cognac? I've just gotten in a bottle of vintage I think you'll like.'

In a cutting tone, I tell him that there are no vintages in cognac. His smile fades. It's nothing against him, but the very idea of lies inspires an uncontrollable rage in me. I can see in his eyes that I have a foreign accent, that *he's* the Frenchman and this is none of my business.

'A Coke,' I say to wipe away the incident. 'With rum.'

'A Cuba Libre,' he translates, tonelessly.

He turns on his heels. I straighten my suit, which was rumpled by the concierge, fold the lapels back down, and tuck in my shirt. My wound hurts; my fingers have swelled even more under the bandages. It's a miracle I got away with just some broken finger bones, repeated the doctors, who attributed it to the accident. But the pain has spread all the way to my neck; I might have something more serious that they haven't picked up on. I was so comfortable in my coma. What I've retained from those seventy-two hours is a feeling of peace, mellow contentment, like when I was a child at Disney World, lying in bed with the sound of the monorail running above the house, the gentle euphoria of flying away to float in the midst of the vacationers trailing above my slumber . . . The effects of Xilanthyl in the IV, the doctor explained.

And then Muriel's face leaning over my bed when I awoke, her smile of joy and relief, her tears dripping onto my cheeks . . . The nervous tension being released. In five years of driving a cab, I was her first accident. A truck trying to merge, lateral impact, knocked against a guardrail, thrown into the Seine. In a cracked, very slow voice she reminded me of these events, stressing her consonants, as people do for the deaf or half-senile old men. If I didn't come out of the coma, she'd vowed never to drive a taxi again. That said, she added frankly, my return to life didn't change her future very much. Class five violation, summons to appear in court, and loss of her driver's license. She let it go at that, but I could easily read the rest in her silence. I recalled certain phrases she'd uttered at my bedside: her prayers for me to open my eyes, her anxiety, her discouragement, all those confidences that had escaped uninhibited from her, since she figured I couldn't hear them. Divorced, raising two kids in some dead-end housing development in the northern suburbs, hog-tied by the long-term loan she'd taken out to buy her taxi shield. A body eaten away by worries, her muscles a bit too prominent beneath her sweater, black hair held back with a comb, weary features with no makeup, eyes that must once have laughed and shown pleasure but now only watched the road. Pretty enough, beneath her bulletproof toughness and her scars. An angel conditioned to withstand anti-tank mines, but with a chink in the armor plating. Apparently she'd brought me back up to the surface single-handedly: none of the witnesses had dived in, thinking it more important to jot down the license of the truck that was speeding from the scene.

When I told her my name, once out of the coma, and that I couldn't reach my wife, she went to verify that I indeed lived at the address I'd given. The door to the building was closed and she'd rung the intercom in vain. Since the doctors had discharged me, but the administrator refused to let me go without getting my insurance information, she practically kidnapped me, calling the hospital imprisonment at a thousand euros a day: she'd drive me home and I could come back to pay the bill when I was ready, and that was that. I couldn't stop thanking her, and she couldn't stop apologizing to me. In the taxi lent by a vacationing co-worker, she drove me to my door. She gave me her card, just in case, and drove off again once she saw me talking into the intercom. In a hurry to forget about me, no doubt, now that I was out of danger.

'We're out of rum,' says the waiter. 'Plain Coke or something else?'

'Plain Coke, then.'

'For cognac, by the way, I just wanted to point out that, legally, we're allowed to label it vintage after 1970, if you've got a certificate from the Bordeaux court, and even before 1970 if you do carbon-dating.'

'My apologies. Let's make it a Coke and cognac.'

His barely civil attitude dissolves in a grinding of jaws. I'm about to ask him where the nearest police station is when I remember that I don't have any money on me. In the time it takes him to get back to his bar, I've vanished.

I spot a policeman across the street, listen to his directions, and thank him. He gives me a smile. I remain there for a moment, as if glued to that smile, with a kind of secret happiness. He doesn't

Didier Van Cauwelaert

know who I am, but he has no cause to doubt me; he trusts me, is giving me credit. My insistent stare lowers his smile. He turns away and goes to deal with a double-parked car.

Suddenly, my reaction frightens me. I have to get hold of myself. Look confident. It's just a bad joke, a marital spat that will soon be resolved. I'm sorry to have to air our private life, but Liz is leaving me no choice.

2

'Do you have any identification?'

Laboring to keep my patience, I explain that I don't, and that's the point: I've come to report them lost.

'Any supporting documents?'

'Yes. But the thing is, they're at my house – that's the second problem. As I was telling your partner before, they're not letting me in.'

The policeman knits his brow, looks over at his partner, but she's gone off to handle something else. They've made me wait for twenty minutes, bouncing me from one window to the next to answer the same questions over and over. At regular intervals, they drag in kids shouting in some foreign language dressed up as skeletons, witches, and pumpkins; their victims rush up to the police officers with an air of priority and I wait for it to be my turn again.

'Are you a French citizen?'

'American.'

'Have you contacted your consulate?'

'Not yet. First I wanted to see if you could help me take care of a problem at home. It's only three blocks away, but your partner said I have to start by filing a complaint.'

'What arrondissement do you live in?'

'The eighth.'

He sighs, annoyed that I fall under his jurisdiction. He's a sunburned redhead who's not pleased to be back from vacation, peeling under the neon lights in front of his screen. He pulls closer to his desk, adjusts his rolling chair in front of the keyboard.

'Name?'

'Harris.'

He waits. I spell it out. He searches for the letters, presses the keys, asks me if I'm related to the bakery chain. I say no.

'First name?'

'Martin.' I say it English-style, pronouncing the *n*.

'Like a woman?'

'No, not Martine, Martin.'

'Written like in French.'

'Right.'

'Occupation?'

'Botanist.'

I start to spell it, but he interrupts sharply that he knows what that is: plants.

'A gardener, in other words,' he translates.

'Not really. I'm director of a research lab at Yale University, and I'm here to work in the Biogenetics Department at the INRA.'

'What's that?'

'National Institute for Agronomic Research, unit 42, 75 Rue Waldeck-Rousseau in Bourg-la-Reine.'

He sighs, taps his index finger on a key to erase what he'd started entering.

'Date of birth?'

'September ninth, 1960.'

'Where?'

'Orlando, Florida.'

'So you're American.'

'Right.'

With a bitter look, he nods toward the children lined up on the benches and points out that Halloween is an American custom. I commiserate as emphatically as I can, to keep him from getting too sidetracked.

'Local address?'

'1 Rue de Duras, Paris 8.'

'So what's your complaint?'

'Identity theft, attempted fraud, false statements, abuse of trust . . .'

'Hold on, there! I've only got two fingers!'

He makes me repeat it, stops to take a call and look through a file. After giving a list of names, he hangs up and turns back to my case, pushing his mouse around the pad.

'And who are you filing against?'

He raises his head after five seconds of silence and repeats his question. I murmur, 'Martin Harris.'

He knits his brow, checks his screen, looks me in the eye again, and says slowly, 'You're bringing charges against yourself?'

'No – against the man who's taken my place. I don't know his real name.'

'Explain.'

'I was in a car accident. I spent six days at Saint-Ambroise hospital, and when I got home I found another man living in my apartment.'

'A squatter?'

'That's one way to put it. He's told all the neighbors he's me.'

'So he's your double.'

'Not in the slightest. But I never had a chance to introduce myself to the others in the building, since I had the accident practically as soon as I arrived. I don't know how he managed it, but he's living an entire life under my name.'

The detective reads what he's typed in, completes my deposition, thinks for a moment. Instinctively, I've chosen not to tell him about Liz. Until now, I've read in his eyes that my story is holding up, and I don't want it to turn into just another adultery case, like before with the concierge. Identity theft is a reasonable cause for complaint. A wife refusing to recognize her spouse in front of witnesses is already a bit shakier.

'Brigitte!'

His partner comes over and he shows her his screen. She leans over, stops chewing her gum for a moment, frowns.

'Doesn't Rue de Duras look out onto the Faubourg?'

'I'm sending somebody.'

'Have a seat while we check into it.'

I nod, surprised by the sudden effectiveness of my enquiry. I walk toward the plastic seats bolted to the wall, but he calls me back.

'Is there anyone who can vouch for you?'

I hesitate.

'The man who owns my apartment. He's a colleague, Dr Paul de Kermeur. He's the one who invited me to come work with him here, and he's lending me an apartment he inherited from his mother . . .'

'Are you renting or borrowing?'

'It depends on how well our work goes. If we decide to make it more long term, I imagine the INRA will cover the rent . . .'

'Do you know his number?'

'060-914-0720.'

I say it with disproportionate pride, but each memory that comes back to me without effort is yet another proof – even if I don't need to prove anything to myself, and I run the risk of making him suspicious with my lesson-well-learned tone.

'Answering machine,' he says, handing me the receiver.

'. . . but please leave a message,' Kermeur's voice continues in my ear, 'and I'll return your call as soon as I can.' *Beep.*

'Hello, Paul, it's Martin Harris. Excuse me for

bothering you, but if you could call me back right away, I'm at . . .'

The redhead lifts his eyes, nods toward the sheet tacked to the wall with the station's main number on it. I read it into my colleague's answering machine. Then I add in the same tone, in response to the question he must be asking himself since reading the latest issue of *Nature*:

'For the hammer orchid, I can confirm that it is indeed pollinated by Thynnidae, and not Gorytini.'

I hand the phone back to the detective, who continues filling in my personal information with no visible reaction. I'm immediately angry at myself for parading my knowledge so obviously that it could look like I'm trying to throw him off the scent. That said, until now he's had no call to put my good faith in doubt.

A terrible bout of anxiety twists my stomach into knots as I go and sit down again, amid the gang of kids who are snickering under their breath in their hermetic language. The aforementioned Brigitte walks up to the three skeletons on my left with a list and a telephone, signals for them to talk to the person on the other end of the line, then takes back the receiver, listens, and calls to the redhead, 'They're not Albanians.'

'Shit. So what's left?'

'Belarus, Bosnia, Estonia . . . ,' the girl recites limply, moving her finger down the list.

'What about Chechnya?' suggests their victim, a fat guy in plaid sitting at the end of the row.

'We don't have an interpreter for that.'

'Goddamn Eastern countries!' the fat man grumbles.

'Eighty per cent of the time,' the girl points out, 'they're French kids who pretend to come from there so we can't do anything to them.'

The mugging victim swallows his prejudices, disappointed, then turns toward me and relates with convivial rancor, over the heads of the three kids, how they picked his pocket while he was photographing the Luxor Obelisk. I nod and turn my eyes away, concentrating on my own problem.

'What about you?' he continues, taking my side. 'What did they steal from you?'

'Everything.'

I say it in a sober tone. He pulls back his chest, looks me over with a perplexed face, and waits for me to say more. I turn away. Brigitte and the redhead, each on the phone, listlessly continue their tour of French interpreters. I hope they're not tying up the switchboard and that a line is still open in case Paul de Kermeur calls back. At the same time, a vague apprehension makes me hope he doesn't. It's insane how quickly you can get used to absurdity. I'm still certain of being me, but I'm becoming less and less sure of everyone else.

An armed squad rushes down the stairs and out of the station. Doors slamming, sirens. I look away. Brigitte goes up to the vending machine, asks the repairman working on it how long it's going to take. He gives a frown of uncertainty. I mechanically begin reviewing my life to prepare for the confrontation, searching for irrefutable arguments that will convince the police. But my doubts grow larger as the minutes tick by. Liz's lover would never have the gall to come here, to claim to be me in front of the police. They won't open the door to the cops, will pretend no one's home, and I'll have no choice but to initiate proceedings at the consulate. Without identity papers, I won't get anywhere.

My hand isn't hurting as much anymore, but my fingers are still very swollen. I try to undo the bandages they put on at the hospital, while the little girl sitting next to me falls asleep against my arm, her face at peace under her witch's makeup.

'How much longer do I have to put up with this farce?' the false me shouts as he comes barreling in.

Closely followed by two policemen, he charges up to the window and slams his hand down, demanding to talk to the superintendent.

'He's not here,' says the redhead. 'And settle down. Your papers!'

I stand up. The stranger takes out a passport that he slaps onto the table, turning a hard face toward me while the detective looks through it.

'Come here, you!'

I walk up, maintaining as natural an expression as possible, despite my racing pulse.

'Martin Harris, huh?' the cop growls, waving the open passport under my nose.

I remain speechless. It has my name, my date and place of birth. And the other man's photo.

'Is this some kind of joke? You think we have nothing better to do?'

'But that's me!' I stammer, gesturing toward the

other. 'Interrogate him! Ask me! You'll see that's not him!'

'That's enough, mister, or we'll throw you in the tank for insulting an officer!'

I raise my hands, assure him that I respect his function and that all I'm asking is for us to unmask this impostor, who on top of everything is carrying a false ID.

'That's your story. This passport looks perfectly legit,' he adds, leafing through it again.

I'm about to demand a full examination, a counterfeit detector, but then I spot the stamp of his arrival in France on the last page, exactly where they put mine last Thursday.

'You satisfied? Good. Now you're going to stop bothering this gentleman, got it?'

'But just think for a minute! Why would I come here to bring charges if I'm not who I say I am?'

'I'm not a shrink.'

I look hard at the blond with gray eyes who's smirking back at me, arms folded, with the superior air of someone who has credence on his side. I hesitate among a thousand details that he couldn't possibly know, then blurt out to the cop, 'Ask him what his father's name is!'

'You said *his* father,' the detective stresses with a victorious smile.

'Franklin Harris,' the other one answers. 'Born on 15 April 1924, in Springfield, Missouri. Died on 4 July 1979, of a cardiovascular collapse at Maimonides Medical Center in Brooklyn.'

'Is that true?' the policeman asks me, seeing my hand clenching the edge of the table.

'How should *he* know?' the other retorts.

I cry out that it wasn't a cardiovascular collapse but an allergy to iodine.

'That caused a collapse!' he immediately adds. 'Who told you about that? You hired a private detective, is that it?'

The knowing look the policeman gives me suddenly makes me lose my footing.

'Careful, don't let him fool you. He's trying to turn things around!'

'My father died from cardiac arrest brought on by anesthesia with iodine as he was about to be operated on for an intestinal blockage,' the stranger recaps, with an authority that takes the words out of my mouth. 'He was participating in a kind of bet among hot-dog eaters when he collapsed . . .'

'That's not true! It wasn't a bet, it was the annual

contest sponsored by Nathan's every July Fourth! My father won three years in a row, and he gave half his winnings to the Coney Island orphanage!'

Complete silence falls on the police station. Everyone is staring at me. I've screamed it out, beside myself. I stammer an apology, stare into the detective's eyes with a sincerity that can't be faked.

'Listen,' he sighs. 'You two work this out outside. We've got other things to do.'

The impostor nods and reaches out to retrieve his passport. I grip his arm and spin him around toward me. 'And what am I working on right now? Why am I in France?'

His eyes don't turn away. On the contrary, he looks straight at me, eyelids narrowing. Like an appeal, a sign of reconciliation, a request for truce. Either he doesn't know the nature of my research, or he's trying to remind me that it's confidential.

'Dr Paul de Kermeur is going to call any minute,' I say, feeling like I've finally scored a point.

He turns away, takes our interlocutor as witness. 'Lieutenant, this individual is very well informed. I don't know how. I don't know if he's an obsessive or a crook, but I want him to stop harassing us!'

'Who's "us"?'

'He showed up a little while ago and started attacking my wife as if she were his.'

'She *is* mine!'

'She has never seen him before. He called her by name and she's very distraught. She's just recovering from a nervous breakdown . . .'

The redhead looks questioningly at the two uniformed cops, who nod. They add that, otherwise, everything is in order. They checked.

'Do you wish to bring charges of harassment, sir?'

His small gray eyes look me over beneath his blond locks. I try to block this insane reversal of the situation by repeating the facts, but the police lieutenant summarizes them: 'This man has identification papers in the name of Martin Harris; you've lost yours. He's married to your wife, which she confirms. And the neighbors all side with him. Have you got anything else to say?'

My lips move without making a sound. He turns toward the other man, asks him again if he wants to press charges.

'No. I have a lot of work to do, and I've wasted enough time on this as it is. I'm perfectly content to put the matter behind us, but he has to leave us alone!'

'You got that? You should thank Mr Harris. But if we catch you near him again, we'll run you in for disturbing the peace! Is that clear?'

The words spin around in my head, stick together, nail me to the spot. I don't even have the strength to throw myself at the stranger as he says goodbye and leaves, hands in his pockets. Free. With my passport. My apartment. My wife. I feel light-headed and grip the table. The others have already forgotten me. My complaint has disappeared from the screen. Erased.

'Are you all right, friend? Would you like to sit down?'

I look at the fat man in plaid who has come up and touched my arm out of genuine concern. From where he was sitting, he must not have understood what was going on. But he senses that I'm innocent, that I'm a victim, like him. He identifies with me, whispers that they'll end up telling him, too, that if the kids robbed him, it's because he provoked them with his wallet.

'Is there anything I can do to help?'

I stammer that I need to make a phone call. He

hands me his cell. Only one person can put an end to this nightmare – unless she doesn't recognize me anymore. The most aberrant behavior starts appearing logical if it gets repeated enough. All these denials have left me unable to defend myself, justify myself. I feel attacked from within, eaten away, dissolved . . . How long can you survive when you no longer exist for anyone?

I start dialing the number, but I've forgotten the last four digits. I check the card in my pocket. With the awful feeling that, if only I lost my memory, everything would fall back into place.

3

The taxi brakes at the curb. The passenger door opens and I climb in.

'Trouble?' asks Muriel, pointing at the police station.

I considered waiting for her inside so that she could give a statement, but they literally threw me out the door, telling me to go get treatment. I stood for ten minutes next to the No Parking sign. No one noticed me, except for one young man who came up to ask for a light. I was pretending to search my pockets when the taxi pulled up.

'What's going on, Martin?'

I shake my head, bite my lips and hold back my tears. A shrill whistle from the sidewalk: they signal her to move on. After about a hundred yards, she asks where to.

'Listen, I don't want you to feel obligated . . . Something terrible has happened and I have no one else to turn to. I'm sorry, but . . . I'm all alone.

I'm in an insane situation and no one will listen to me.'

'Go on, I'm just hitting the meter. So what's the problem?'

I take a deep breath and recap in a few sentences what I've been through since she dropped me off at my building. Someone honks us. The light has turned green; she starts up again and goes past the intersection to park.

'Wait a second, Martin. This guy claims to be you, he's carrying a passport with your name on it, and your wife is living with him?'

'Right,' I say, hoping that her dynamic tone of voice is about to lead to some miraculous explanation.

'And no one in your building recognizes you.'

'That's correct.'

She turns away and scratches the steering wheel for a moment before adding in a small voice while staring through the windshield, 'And you've just come out of a three-day coma, after a head injury.'

'What's that got to do with it? I'm the same guy as before the accident. You're a witness. You're the only one who . . .'

I stop.

'Who what?' she encourages me, visibly eager to hear any argument in my favor.

With a lump in my throat, I shake my head. My last hope has crumbled into dust.

'You're not a witness to anything. I didn't tell you my name until after I woke up. The only thing you know about me before the accident is that I was going to Charles-de-Gaulle and I was in a hurry.'

Her silence confirms the objection that, in any case, she would have ended up making herself. I sense all too well that she can believe only in one thing, my sincerity. And if I lose her trust, I'm left with nothing.

'So apparently,' she summarizes, 'you have no way of proving that he isn't you.'

'So what does that mean?' I say with a harshness that I don't even try to hide. 'That I've got amnesia? You can see for yourself that isn't the case. I'm the opposite of an amnesiac, I remember *everything*.'

'Maybe you just think you remember . . . And you've forgotten who you really are . . .'

She says this in a very gentle voice, with the standard precautions, the required abruptness: the voice one uses out of moral honesty and human respect to make a patient understand that he's done for. Then she puts her hand on my arm and says, to finish me off with kindness, 'It happens sometimes.'

'Sure.'

The cold determination in my voice startles her. I ask her to lend me her cell phone. She watches me dial the number, which I remember effortlessly.

'What if we go back to the hospital, Martin? What I told you was just my feeling, a hypothesis, but I don't really know. Maybe the doctors have already come across cases like this . . .'

'Of course. You come out of a coma and poof! you believe you're someone else. With his memories, his profession, his personality, his problems . . .'

'Listen, I really want to believe you, but I have nothing to compare against. You said so yourself, I didn't know you *before*.'

'How do I put this thing on speaker?'

She presses a green button. A pre-recorded musical soundtrack invites us to please stay on the line.

'Muriel . . . Just give me a chance to convince you, just two minutes. If I can't, you can take me back to the hospital and I'll let them lock me away. Okay?'

'I just said that to . . .'

'American Express, this is Virginia speaking.'

'This is 4937 0843 12 75009, expiration 6/06.'

Muriel stares at me attentively. I look back at her, holding my breath.

'How can I help you, Mr Harris?'

We smile at each other spontaneously. She looks as relieved as I am, freed from the legitimate doubts I'd inspired. I'm glad to see she's happy that I'm not insane. She still feels responsible for my accident, despite all the problems it's causing her.

'I've lost my card,' I say into the cell phone that I'm holding between us, on the armrest. 'I'd like to cancel it and get a new one.'

'Very good, sir. May I ask you a few questions?'

'Go ahead.'

She asks me for my place and date of birth, my mother's maiden name. I answer in a natural, detached, mechanical tone of voice.

'Your permanent address?'

'255 Sawmill Lane, Greenwich, Connecticut. But I'm currently living in Paris at 1 Rue de Duras in the eighth . . .'

'Very good. Would you like to receive your new card at that address?'

'No, absolutely not!'

My outburst makes the phone fall off the armrest. Muriel picks it up and hands it back to me.

'To what address then, sir?'

I give her a questioning look. She hesitates for five seconds, then articulates slowly, 'Nouméa building, Îles development, Clichy 92110. Care of Muriel Caradet.'

I repeat the address, wrinkling my eyelids in thanks.

'And there you go,' I say, putting down the phone. 'Forgive me for taking advantage like this . . . As soon as I get my card, I'm taking you out to the best restaurant in Paris.'

The warmth in my voice immediately cools her off. The euphoria we briefly shared, as I was proving my identity while cutting off the impostor's resources, gives way to a different sort of discomfort. Maybe she thinks I'm just trying to pick her up. I try to think how to dissipate the misunderstanding without seeming crass.

'That doesn't prove anything, Martin.'

'What doesn't?'

'I mean, it doesn't prove that you're any more authentic than the other guy. You could have seen his Amex number and memorized it, like the rest of his information. What I've just seen you do, pardon me for saying so, but it could also be simple credit card fraud.'

I spread out my hands and let them fall, completely deflated.

'Please understand, I'm not calling you a liar. But you haven't gotten any further than when the police didn't believe you.'

I let myself fall back against the seat, close my eyes. She adds that she's sorry, but she still thinks the best thing is to go back to the hospital. I bring my hand down sharply on the armrest.

'But why would I do this? If all I wanted was to steal somebody's credit card, why would I do it in front of you? When all I have to do is take you to the INRA in Bourg-la-Reine, and it would take me two minutes to prove I'm a well-known botanist back in the States! You can find my work on the internet, and surely somewhere there's my photo . . .'

'Well, then, let's go!' she snaps. 'And if it turns

out not to be your photo, you'll just say he hacked into the site.'

'Do you have any other explanation?' I shoot back, furious that she's put us in a position of failure from the start, that in the sweep of her logic she's formulated a hypothesis I hadn't even thought of.

'Yes I do! You might have read an article about him just before the accident . . .'

'That's right, an article that gave his Amex number!'

'Listen, Martin, I don't know which way is up anymore! I want to help you, but there are limits!'

'Montparnasse station,' a guy says, getting in.

He settles into the back seat and pulls the door shut. Muriel turns around to tell him she isn't free.

'It's pouring!' he answers. 'I've been cooling my jets for an hour and not a single cab has stopped. Give me a break, would you, please . . .'

'It's fine,' I say, opening my door. 'Just lend me a euro for the bus. I'll pay you back as soon as . . .'

'You won't get very far on one euro.'

'My train is leaving in twenty minutes,' the guy says impatiently.

'I don't give a shit about your train!' Muriel

shouts. 'I'm talking! Stay here, you,' she segues, closing my door again. 'Fine, I'll take you to Bourg-la-Reine and we'll drop this one off at Montparnasse. It's on the way.'

I get thrown back against the seat as she peels away.

'Thank you,' says the passenger.

While she slaloms through traffic, he makes call after call to reassure his correspondents and push back the time of his meeting in Nantes in case he misses his train. The rhythm of his guttural voice repeating the same thing over and over, with slight inflections of deference or superiority, isolates me in a bubble that helps me clear my head. I shut my eyes and let myself drift, trying to catch my breath. Hearing someone spend so much energy explaining problems other than mine, and such insignificant ones at that, is somehow comforting.

'Other than your website, what could make me change my mind?'

I open my eyes, note bitterly that it only took a mile or two of reflection for her to side with the enemy camp.

'Muriel, my wife is the one who set this all up. I can't think of any other explanation. She learned about my accident, thought I was dead, and passed her lover off as me . . .'

'Wouldn't it be simpler just to be a widow?'

I can't think of an answer, so I pursue my thoughts alone. Liz might have erased me from her married life and imposed her accomplice on the neighbors, but that's where it ends: he could never get away with it in Bourg-la-Reine. A fake passport and memories learned by heart won't be enough; you can't improvise twenty years of research and exploration. They can't replace me professionally overnight.

'My colleague Paul de Kermeur brought me to France so we could pool our research. He spent hours corresponding with me by email. He knows all my studies on the intelligence of plant life. They won't be able to fool *him*!'

'Five minutes early, great!' the guy in back rejoices. 'How much?'

'Nineteen ten,' answers Muriel, showing the meter that was running for me.

He hands her a twenty, tells her to keep the change, and rushes into the station with his attaché case. She tries to give me the bill, but I refuse. She reminds me that I have nothing on me and says I can pay her back for the ride when I get my new card. The ease with which she has come back to my side leaves me disarmed. I pocket the bill.

'I'm sorry I got angry, Muriel.'

She pulls a gray plastic sheath from the glove compartment and gets out of the car. A small thump on the roof. She sits back down and hands me her cell.

'Since you're already racking up debts, why don't you call the States? Your family, or a friend . . .'

'My father is dead and I don't know where my mother is. Apart from my wife, I only have acquaintances, or co-workers . . . And it's four in the morning over there.'

'Have it your way,' she says, rummaging behind the meter. 'But that seemed the easiest solution to me. You let me talk to the person, I'll give them your description, and I'll see if it's actually you.'

I swallow my saliva, disappointed that she still needs this kind of verification. But she's right. I ask if she speaks English.

'A little.'

'I'll call Rodney Cole, my assistant at Yale.'

On the third ring, a synthetic voice tells me that

the person is not available. Muriel takes back the phone and shuts it off with a sigh.

'I can try waking somebody else up.'

'No, don't bother. Now it's in the call log and I can call him myself if I have any doubts. This way I'll see if you dialed a real number or not.'

She starts off again. I look at the traffic, huddled in my seat. After a moment, she puts her hand on my knee.

'I want to believe you, Martin. But I've been lied to so many times in my life. What street in Bourg-la-Reine?'

4

We enter a lobby made of black glass and decorated with a dying yucca in the middle of a Zen garden.

'Hello,' I say to the receptionist.

'Mr . . . ?'

'Mr Harris.'

'He's not here. Who shall I say wanted to see him?'

I grit my teeth and avoid looking at Muriel, laboring to preserve my calm, politeness, and sense of obviousness when I answer. '*He* is me!'

She studies me, brows knit, as if she were searching her memory.

'Sorry, I just took over for Nicole and I don't know everyone yet. Your name was . . . ?'

'No, you don't understand. *I* am Mr . . .'

'Is Paul de Kermeur here?' Muriel cuts in.

'No, ma'am, he won't be in until three, either.'

She starts to look away, but I grab her arm.

'That's not true. He's in his lab. He does his

47

experiments every morning alone and he doesn't want to be disturbed. Miss, would you please call him, extension 6310? Tell him it's an urgent matter regarding the Thynnidae, from Martin Harris.'

'Regarding the what?'

'Thynnidae. It's a kind of wasp – he'll understand.'

With her tongue in the corner of her lips, she pushes some buttons and murmurs into her headphone, 'Sir, it's a gentleman for the wasps, sent by Mr Harris. Very well.'

She smiles and says in an air-stewardess voice that I can go ahead. I stay where I am, my toes curled in my shoes. She looks at me quizzically.

I ask, 'I believe it's across the way?'

'Sorry, yes. You go back out and it's across the road, the tan building marked Unit 42. I'll unlock the gate for you.'

As we cross the street, I explain to Muriel that Dr de Kermeur has a fairly special position at the INRA. A number of his colleagues reproach him for working at the crossroads of genetics, molecular biology, and the paranormal. That said, they mainly resent that he actually makes discoveries, which in France seems to be incompatible with the status of researcher.

'Back home, he'd be a university department head, with half a million a year in funding. Here, they're just waiting out his retirement by sticking him in some prefab shack behind the trash bins.'

She watches me pass through the electrified fence, which shuts behind us, cross the parking lot in long strides. I breathe easier as I find my bearings. Finally. Even though this is the first time I've set foot here, I feel at home. I recognize the surroundings that Kermeur described in his emails, the kind of construction shed in which he persists in trying to prove that plant DNA is related to the golden section, and that the introduction of any new gene is a catastrophe of unimaginable proportions. Muriel holds me back at the door to the shed.

'Go gently. He's already working with the other one, you heard her. Don't go in there saying, 'Hi, I'm the real Martin.' Play it cool. Let him come to you to keep him from digging in his heels.'

I smile at her in the rain. She moves me, with her messily cut hair sticking to her hollow cheeks and her eyes that are used to seeing problems,

danger, scams. Traffic jams, complainers, passengers who come on to her, late-night attacks,
kids to watch between runs . . . She copes with all
of it, and none of it seems to get to her. The speed
with which she passes from justifiable suspicion
to freely given trust, from angry outburst to tact,
touches me well beyond the immediate circum-
stances. She's an only child, like me, who must
have grown up nurturing a dream that never came
true but has remained intact, and prevents the drab
colors of her life from bleeding into her. I followed
my childhood vocation, without ever straying
from the path. I accomplished everything I set out
to do, and now I find myself utterly bereft in the
face of betrayal, abandonment, lies . . . Liz has
always been a liar. She was a lawyer before we met,
but her beauty helped me forget all that. I didn't
want to see the cracks beneath the veneer, the
instability behind her strength of character, the
misunderstandings hidden by silences, the fragility
masked by her unassailable indifference. How
badly she must have hated me to reach this point.
Was I really so obsessed with my plants? Maybe
this was her only way of letting me know that she
exists, independent, available, and still young,

that she can't stand me anymore and that I'm replaceable.

'Should we go in, or would you rather we get drenched first?'

I apologize and press the buzzer above the label marked 'Unit 42'. A sputter, then the door opens.

'Come in,' Paul de Kermeur calls out from his microscope. 'Let me just finish this observation and I'll be right with you.'

He doesn't look at all like what I'd imagined. I'd pictured a mandarin embittered by persecutions, crew cut, stiff as a board, square glasses. Instead, he's an anxious little man with a gray ponytail, wearing a sailor's sweater and hip-hop pants.

'Why did Harris tell me it was Gorytini if it's Thynnidae?'

I swallow my answer. Muriel told me to go slow.

'I had them shipped all the way from Australia!' he says with audible annoyance.

I confirm that it's the Thynnidae that pollinate the *Drakea*. He detaches a red-ringed eye from his microscope.

'*Drakea*? I thought it was the hammer orchid!'

'It's the same plant. It was named after Miss Drake, the English botanist who wondered how it managed to reproduce when its pollen didn't attract any insects.'

'Did she think it was the wind, like Darwin?'

'That's not entirely wrong, insofar as the wind helps it spread the pheromones of female Thynnidae.'

'But it could also attract the Gorytini.'

'No, Paul. Mimetic labelli only attract males of like species. That monogamy explains why the hammer orchid never makes any hybrids.'

I meet Muriel's gaze as she watches us in turn, squinting and biting her lips. Her jubilation at realizing she was right to trust me takes years off her face.

'Don't translate, whatever you do,' she whispers in my ear. 'I love it.'

'Just a moment, let me check the reactions and then I'm all yours,' my colleague says, burying his face in the microscope once more. 'Have a seat.'

I pull Muriel across a jumble of file folders, electrical cables, insect cages, and plant samples crammed between the mattresses and metal cabinets. I clear off part of a chair for her and sit down on a stack of books.

'So Thynnidae and Gorytini are what, some kind of wasp?' Muriel summarizes.

I tell her to forget about Gorytini: I spent six months in the Australian bush proving that Miss Drake had been mistaken.

'And what do Thynnidae look like?'

'Like ants. They feed on beetle larvae that live parasitically on the roots. This means they have to live underground, and because of that they've lost their wings, which couldn't help them dig subterranean tunnels. They only come out when it's time to reproduce, to attract a mate by climbing onto a flower.'

'The hammer orchid.'

'No. Only the male Thynnidae interests the orchid, because he's kept his wings. So to attract him, the orchid has devised an ingenious stratagem: it recreates the odor of the female, before she has even come out from underground. Her imitated sexual pheromones imbibe the pollen stem; the male dives in to copulate, wriggles about in vain, and leaves frustrated when he realizes he's been had. Frustrated but covered in pollen, which he transports to other flowers – and the trick has been successful.'

'That orchid's a real cow.'

'Just survival instinct.'

'And that took you six months to figure out.'

'It lasts less than a second. False copulation. No one had ever observed it or captured it on film. What Paul's trying to do is recreate the process in the laboratory on a genetically modified *Drakea*, to measure the influence of the mutation on the Thynnidae's behavior.'

'So the guy who's claiming to be you got the wrong wasp.'

'That proves one thing: he's read the latest issue of *Nature*. I was looking at it on the plane. A researcher at Oxford wrote up my discovery without citing me, on top of which she confused Gorytini with Thynnidae.'

'Everyone's ripping you off, in other words.'

I grab her wrist in a rush of nerves.

'Do you believe me, Muriel?'

She replies with a vague gesture.

'I never finished high school, the farthest I've ever traveled is Corsica, and I'm allergic to bee stings. So you could tell me anything . . .'

She raises a hand so that I'll let her finish.

'. . . but I find all this amusing, and interesting,

and it rings true. There you go. You're a scientist, that much is obvious. I don't know if you're who you say, but at least you're that.'

I swallow my saliva and tell her thank you.

'You do me more good than you know, Muriel. You can only be called a liar so many times before you start doubting the truth . . . I didn't think it was possible.'

'Tell me about it. My ex made up so many stories about me during the divorce, it took me months to repair the damage. The more I tried to explain to my kids, the less they believed me. In the end I was forced to lie just to sound credible. When I got my daughter back, she was practically suicidal. Don't think I've become involved in your problems just because I drove you into the Seine.'

I lower my eyes and nod.

'So, you're a friend of Martin's,' says Paul de Kermeur, walking toward us.

Re-energized by Muriel's words, I leap to my feet and say, 'No.' She grabs my left hand and squeezes my fingers so that I'll take it easy.

'It's fascinating working with him,' he continues, ignoring my answer.

'Have you been working together long?'

'Six days. And even then, he's only come here once, he's been sick. A sore throat he picked up on the flight over.'

'Of course,' I say, with a knowing look toward Muriel. 'He can't talk, so he won't give himself away.'

'Give himself away?'

I stare him in the face with the friendliest look I can muster, rest my hands on his shoulders, and recite to him the last email I sent him from Yale. He interrupts, pointing at me.

'You're Rodney, his assistant.'

'No, I'm him. Or rather, he's trying to pass himself off as me.'

'What?'

Muriel takes over, tells him about the accident, my awakening in the hospital, my discovery of a stranger wearing my pajamas. He listens to all this with raised eyebrows, forehead in ripples, then turns toward me.

'Is this your wife?'

'No, my wife is with him.'

His ponytail comes undone. He quickly gathers his hair in his fist, twists it, and ties it back up.

'I've seen Mrs Harris!'

'When you handed her the keys to the apartment at the Café des Galeries,' I quickly add, so as not to give him time to doubt me. 'The day we arrived. I'd just hopped into this woman's cab to return to the airport, because I'd left my computer . . . By the way, Paul, when you saw him, was he carrying a PowerBook?'

'Huh? Uh, yes, I think so . . . Wait a minute. Are you saying that I've been working with an impostor?'

'Would you agree to tell that to the police?'

'Why not to the newspapers, while we're at it! Sure! I waste the taxpayers' money by involving the INRA in a series of joint experiments with an impostor!'

He drops onto a crate, deflated.

'Who would do such a thing to me? It couldn't be Topik, could it?'

'Topik who?'

'The Nobel winner. He accused me of fraud in *Le Monde*, when I demonstrated that genetic modifications in corn mess up the DNA Supracode and can lead to the generation of new viruses. We're government employees, here at the INRA;

that means he's implicating me in abuse of funds. I slapped him with a libel suit, so he's been trying to discredit me any way he can . . . But even so . . .' He resumes three seconds later, his voice lower: 'Your story doesn't hold water.'

I point out that it's *his* story. He stands up vehemently.

'But still, you can't just pass yourself off as someone else that easily! There are identity papers, fingerprints . . . No? What? What did I say?'

'Thank you. I hadn't thought about fingerprints.'

I whisper to Muriel that I'll go get them at the consulate, so they can be compared. Surely they must be on file somewhere in the States.

'And besides,' Kermeur says suddenly, grabbing my sleeve. 'What if it's *you* who's trying to con me, and you're the one passing himself off as Martin Harris?'

Muriel breaks in to certify that the other one started it, and then she turns toward me, her mouth crooked. No doubt she's just realized that all she knows about my confrontations with him is what I've told her. Seeing the two of them staring at me like fish waiting for food behind the glass is enough to give me a stroke.

'Listen, there's no point in arguing about it. Call that man, Paul, and make him come here, sore throat or not – anyway, I saw him not an hour ago and his voice was fine, he was perfectly healthy! Tell him something important has come up, and whatever you do, don't mention me or he'll get suspicious.'

'Wait a minute, wait a minute . . . How do I know you're not a spy for Monsanto?'

I stare at him open-mouthed. Muriel asks who that is.

'A multinational that's marketing GMOs – that's genetically modified foods to you – supposedly to combat world hunger, but really to control the worldwide market with grains that have to be bought again every year!'

He stabs his finger at me and explains to her, getting more and more heated with every sentence, that I could have been sent by Monsanto to learn how far he and Martin have gotten in their experiments on the dangers of GMOs.

'You don't really think we're going to reveal all that to you, do you?' he continues, advancing toward me. 'That would be too easy! Your bosses will have to come up with another plan to find out what's in store for them!'

'Cut it out, Paul. I know *everything*, okay? I know everything because it's me. If anyone is working for Monsanto, it's the guy who's trying to take my place, and maybe you're right, maybe that's it . . .'

'I refuse to take that risk! Get out of here!'

'No, listen, you're the one in control, you're the one who'll decide! You'll have us both right in front of you and you can square us off against each other. You know most of my work – you'll be able to tell who's the genuine article.'

'This is insane,' he sighs, wiping his forehead on the back of his sleeve. 'I've got to finish my presentation to the Medical Academy. I don't have time for . . .' He stops, looks me in the eye, and says slowly, 'How did I first hear about your work?'

'It was during a murder trial in Wisconsin, when the judge ruled to allow plants as witnesses. You read my testimony on the internet, how I was able to determine the guilty party, and you contacted me.'

He folds his arms, raises his right hand, and bites his fingernail, never taking his eyes off me.

'Keep going.'

I search for the one detail that will bring him definitively to my side, but I realize that with the

Net, anyone can gain access to anything. Even so, the reporters covering the case must have left out certain details that only I could know.

'There had been a crime in a greenhouse. No witnesses, three possible suspects. I suggested to the judge that we attach my electrodes to the hydrangeas, and we paraded twelve people in front of them, one after another, including the three suspects. Suddenly the needle on the galvanometer started going crazy in front of the victim's brother. It wasn't that the plants had sent out an electric signal to help bring him to justice – they couldn't care less. But he and the victim had grappled in the greenhouse, there had been some broken stems, and the aggressor revived the trauma, triggering a system of electrochemical alert from one hydrangea to the other. Under the shock, the killer confessed.'

I stare into Muriel's eyes as I finish my story.

'That's unbelievable,' she murmurs.

Kermeur signals impatiently for her to be quiet and snaps at me, 'What do I expect to get out of working with you?'

'Proof of double contamination. You believe that genetically modified plants would accelerate their mutations and communicate them to the normal plants around them, which would then defend themselves with a gaseous signal, and that signal in turn would further increase the speed of incoherent mutations in GMOs.'

'What am I basing that on?'

'My experiments on heightened tannin levels in acacia leaves in response to antelope attacks.'

'Where do we differ?'

'The only mutations I've observed are responses to external stimuli. But so far nothing has led me to conclude that the insertion of a gene to ward off meal moths is dangerous enough to modify the DNA. On the other hand, I proved that it was totally useless: corn can already protect itself by creating a gaseous message that attracts predators of the meal moth, but pesticides prevent this message from spreading. If we do away with genetic modifications and pesticides, corn will again be able to protect itself, at no cost and no risk.'

'What's my nephew's name?'

I look at him, at a loss. I rack my brain, run through lists of names. The suspense in Muriel's eyes and the ticking of the wall clock give off the pathetic atmosphere of a television game show.

'Well?' he says impatiently.

'Hold on,' Muriel protests. 'He got all your experiments point for point . . .'

'That doesn't prove anything – he could have hacked into our emails and memorized them. It's the intimate details that tell the story, the ones no one thinks are important. So what's my nephew's name?'

'I'm thinking . . .'

'And yet, I talked about him all the time,' he insists, his face contorted.

'Yes, I know . . . He's thirteen, you've raised him since his parents' accident, he doesn't get along with your new wife, he's no good in math but terrific in Spanish, he's going out with a girl called Charlotte . . .'

'You remember all that?' says Kermeur, surprised.

The new sympathy with which he listens to me raises my nervous tension by a notch.

'. . . one of his three hamsters is sick and he's treating it with antibiotics. He himself refuses to take anything homeopathic, just to stick it to you – those were your words. Right now he's at camp in the Haute-Savoie, he writes to say that he's stuffing his face with GMOs at every meal, but when it comes to his name, I'm sorry, I'm drawing a blank . . . So what's your conclusion? That I'm an agent for Monsanto? All I can come up with is a bogus first name.'

He picks up the phone and dials a number taped to the wall. I walk closer. The impostor's cell phone has the same prefix as the one I lost in the Seine. Liz bought him a prepaid.

'Martin Harris? Hello, it's Kermeur. I hope you're feeling better. Listen, I need to see you right away, there's an administrative inspection by the INRA head office. They need your signature on the project authorization and a letter of intent for information exchange with Yale. I'll be waiting.' Then, to me: 'He's coming,' he says, hanging up. His voice is very neutral. Then he looks at Muriel and continues in a sad, small voice, 'Aurelien. A lovely name, don't you think? My sister came up with it.'

Half an hour has gone by. Sitting in a corner of the lab with food trays, we listen to Paul de Kermeur's woes while munching on cafeteria chicken. I've tried my best to bring the conversation back to me, but he's avoiding the subject, saying he doesn't want me to influence him: he has to maintain his impartiality to catch me out. The phrase sticks in my throat. Like many unhappy souls, Kermeur has an unrepentant egotism, a sincere lack of interest in other people's problems, and not the slightest conscience about boring his listeners to tears. He has pummeled us successively with his sister's death agony, the insecurities of schoolboys, the effect of antibiotics on puberty, and the disarray of the Socialist Party, in which he's been campaigning in vain for the past twenty years for an increase in research credits. Passing from resigned desolation to bilious revolt, he moves from topic to topic with the apparent aim of not letting me get a word in, and of not having to think. No doubt this is his concept of impartiality.

'Ah, there he is!' he cries out, hearing the electric bell.

He leaps to his short legs, runs to push the lock release, pulls up his baggy pants, and reties his ponytail, as if he were the one about to stand trial. I exchange a worried glance with Muriel, seek out her hand under the table. I meet only her knee, which she moves away. I don't take my eyes off her. She stares at the tall blond who has just come in and barely hides her surprise – not to say her preference. I know the comparison isn't in my favor: he is as brilliant as I am dull. Impeccably dressed, elegant, tanned, a precise robot giving off all the self-confidence that I lack. I seem like such a rough draft next to him . . . Following Muriel's reactions out of the corner of my eye, I can feel how much better he plays the part of me than I do. *He* doesn't need to open his mouth in order to be convincing: he looks like a Martin Harris.

'So,' the biogeneticist begins calmly, 'you've got a double?'

The other man freezes in the middle of the cages, looks at me and grinds his teeth. I slowly stand up. I wipe my mouth with the paper napkin, very calm, settled, master of the situation. He turns wholly toward Kermeur: 'Now I understand why you called. Ms Pontaut didn't know anything about an inspection.'

'You talked to Jacqueline Pontaut?'

'I went to the head office, thinking you might be there . . .'

Kermeur blanches. In two seconds, he's lost his advantage, his control, his impartiality. He listens without a peep to the bastard suggest he call security: I'm a lunatic who has been following him, claiming to be him. The police already picked me up, but this time he's going to press charges. Kermeur spins toward me. All that's left in his eyes is fury at having attracted the attention of the administrative services for nothing.

'Are you happy now?' he shouts at me with a kind of hatred.

'Ask him what degrees he holds.'

Then, for the first time, I see the impostor lose some of his self-assurance. He appeals to Kermeur, on the verge of losing it: 'I've had it up to *here* having to show my passport every time I run into this nutcase! Where's it going to be the next time – the supermarket? The tennis club? At the dentist's?'

'Answer him, Martin,' Kermeur advises him, and I have no further illusions about his choice.

'Master of Forestry from Yale University,' he recites. 'Laboratory director since 1990 at the Environmental Science Center, 21 Sachem Street, again at Yale. Ph.D. thesis on plant mutations in the pollination process. Botanical explorations in Australia, Malaysia, the Amazon, and South Africa. Fifteen publications, including a study on electrochemical transmission during herbivore predation . . . Will that do?'

'Why do antelopes die of hunger in nature reserves?' Kermeur shoots at him, picking up the relay.

'Because the vegetation they graze on emits a gaseous message that renders the flora toxic over a radius of six meters.'

'What gas?'

'Ethylene. If the antelopes don't have a large enough territory to get around this chain reaction, they'll let themselves die of starvation rather than poison themselves!'

'Well?' spits Kermeur, spinning toward me with a referee's arrogance.

I shrug my shoulders. I've proved it in five countries, just as I demonstrated the way that certain predators anticipate the response, like the Mexican squash beetle that every day eats a leaf six and a half meters from its last meal – you only have to read my articles to know this. I add that he'd do better to test us about a discovery that hasn't been published yet. Without batting an eyelash, he asks me what change in amino acids causes modifications in the functional sequence of a gene. I have no idea. He turns toward the other, who doesn't know either and points out that that's *his* specialty.

'That's true, my apologies. What's my nephew's name?'

'Aurelien.'

Doing away with the middleman, I ask the impostor which wasp pollinates the hammer orchid.

'Gorytini. More specifically, male Gorytini.'

I correct his mistake, throw the references of my publications in his face. Without losing a beat, he remarks to Kermeur that Gorytini and Thynnidae are two varieties of the same wasp. Floored by his nerve, I deny that ridiculous claim, but he replies by accusing me of deflecting the subject onto insects to hide my gaps in botany.

'Fine, then what is the special characteristic of the *Acacia cornigera*?'

'It hosts colonies of ants and secretes a special pulp for their babies at the tips of its leaves, made up of proteins and fats. Because of this, the ants protect it against aggressors and nourish it in return with insect larvae. How did I prove it?' he shoots back.

'I made the larvae radioactive so I could trace their absorption by the acacia's tissues. When was that?'

'June '96. How do climbing plants manage to orient themselves toward a support?'

'That's something you can't possibly know: I haven't said anything about it, I'm still in the observation stage . . .'

'Which proves that you don't know about my ongoing experiments,' he snickers.

'On the Chilean bignonia? Its tendrils possess papillae that emit . . .'

'. . . that *might* emit gaseous hormones . . .'

'. . . with a reflux that is supposed to bring information about the location of the support back to the papillae.'

'What are the last wooded regions in Malaysia that haven't yet been deforested?'

'Sungai Ureu, Sungai Batu, and Ulu Magoh. I've been campaigning on behalf of the nomad inhabitants of those areas to try to save their living space. What was the government's answer?'

'That they'll have to change their way of life and not be so dependent on the forest; that it was doing them a favor.'

We catch our breath, looking each other over. The other two have followed the confrontation like a tennis match. They glance at each other in silence. It breaks my heart, but if this weren't about me, I'd have to admit that we're equally matched. Liz would never have been able to brief her lover this thoroughly. She doesn't know a thing about botany and cares less: the hypothesis that she's made me an alter ego out of revenge crumbles to dust. This guy is as authentic as I am. He's had the same training and knows all there is to know about the same subjects that I've studied. It's taken me dozens of years to learn all this. How could he come out of nowhere with all that baggage in six days? Unless it's possible that my replacement was already planned, that an agricultural corporation as powerful as Monsanto devised this means of blocking my partnership with Paul de Kermeur to neutralize our campaign against GMOs.

'How did you become so passionate about plants?' Kermeur asks, addressing both of us.

We answer, constantly interrupting each other, that we were born in Orlando and that Dad was a gardener at Disney World. We grew up in a huge playing field where nature was the greatest attraction of all. I shout out suddenly:

'What's the first thing he taught us?'

I can't get over what I've just said: here I am talking to him as if we were twins. He remains silent, staring at me, seeking the answer in my eyes.

'To love snakes,' he finally murmurs. 'To keep plants from being asphyxiated.'

'Why?' Muriel asks him.

I have a knot in my throat. He explains, using the same words I would have used, that snakes eat mosquito larvae, which means fewer treatments with insecticides that prevent the leaves from breathing. I can still see Dad making me handle my first serpent, in the clumps of hibiscus and giant bamboo around the Polynesian Hotel. I remember him cutting endless Mickey Mouses in the shrubbery, Snow Whites out of hawthorn, Donald Ducks in privet. I remember him in front of his personal creation, the enchanted brooms from *Fantasia*, the ends of their ivy arms spilling pails full of forget-me-nots that flooded the lawns of the Magic Kingdom – a composition that earned him the title Employee of the Month. And then I remember him losing weight, letting himself go after Mom left him, starting to drink and not shaving, until Disney had to fire him. I see us moving to Brooklyn, to live near the ocean with an elderly cousin who agreed to take us in. I recall him sinking further and further as the years went by, ending up as watchman for the big Figure-8 roller coaster at Coney Island. I see the shame in his eyes across the table, me behind my schoolbooks and him behind his beers. Double shame: shame for the spectacle he's offering me and the shame he thinks he causes me in front of others. Tell him as I might that I loved him, and that I was proud of him when he won the Nathan's Hot-Dog Eating Contest every year, he couldn't let go of it. Up to the day when he dropped dead while finishing his fourteenth sausage on the hundredth second, posthumously beating his own record – three days before I received the letter from Yale accepting me on scholarship, his last dream on earth . . . All those moments that rise in my throat while the other relates them, without a pause, like so many proofs to his credit. It's horrible. Hearing my life coming out of this guy's mouth. The feeling that everything I know, everything I experience, has been projected out of my head, poured into someone smarter, more open, newer, the way you decant wine into a carafe, and at the bottom of the bottle there's only a murky deposit.

A woman comes in holding a file, asks for some clarifications. They tell her. They no longer care about me. I feel emptied out. My childhood, my work, my memories . . . He knows as much about them as I do. Except that *he* has a passport to back up his claims. And Liz chose him. What good is it to resist, try to convince them? My arm hurts, and so does my head. I no longer have the strength to fight.

'Help me, quick!' cries Muriel.

In a spinning fog, I feel myself being lifted, carried.

'Should I call a doctor?'

'Thanks, no need . . . Just help me get him into the taxi. I'm taking him to the hospital.'

'The hospital.'

'I *told* you he was a psychopath, Paul! The kind that clings to you, copies everything you do, wants the same car, the same job, the same wife . . .'

'But still, Martin, there were things he said . . .'

'Personally, I can't understand why hospitals ever let people like that out!'

'Ms Pontaut is absolutely right: they can turn violent.'

'Be careful, Mr Harris! It's already happened, I saw it in the newspaper: people who were so envious of others that one day they killed them to take their place . . .'

The rest is lost in the bustle of being carried away. To forget. Go back into a coma. That's all I want. To be alone. To be real. To be me.

5

The hospital is quiet, drowsy around its bare garden, just like when I left it this morning. Most of the wards are closed, having been relocated to a more modern, less human structure. Muriel adds that she spent the summer of '98 in this garden, under the window where they were treating her daughter. Her voice carries the same nostalgia as if she were talking about a vacation home she was forced to sell. I listen and say nothing. I act as if I were normal, as if I were docile, as if I were going to heal.

The neuropsychiatrist is expecting us, having been alerted by phone. I insist on going first to the billing office to prove that I'm solvent, give my Amex number and explain my situation. The employee kindly answers that there's no urgency. They're all convinced I'll be here a long time. It's the only solution to the problem I incarnate. Martin Harris cannot live in duplicate. He exists without me; all that's left for me to do is go back to sleep.

'Remember what I told you in the car, Martin.'

I nod. She told me so many things. She's sure I'm the real one. The other guy gave her an uneasy feeling, the impression of being some kind of manufactured product, of soullessly repeating facts learned by heart, while I moved her every time I spoke, and even more when I didn't, while he was reciting his part. She's certain that I'm still having a reaction to the tetanus vaccine. My fainting spell from before was nothing serious, the doctor could reassure me about that, and, if I felt like it, I had her address; she'd set an extra place for dinner, and would like me to meet her children. She spoke slowly, repeated the same words as the streets went by. She sounded sincere, but it was so that I'd go along without a fuss and let them shut me in. She kisses me on the cheeks.

'This evening, then?'

'If all goes well. Thanks.'

'Everything will be fine. I have complete faith: he's a terrific guy. He saved my daughter's life.'

She leaves very quickly. I remain standing in the waiting room, eyes fixed on the taxi as it maneuvers its way out. I'll never see her again. I'll never leave this place.

'Mr Harris?'

I wait a beat, then turn around and say yes. The secretary leads me to the office of the old gentleman with a lamb's head who was smiling serenely when I awoke from my coma. I'll never forget his welcoming sentence, the first words of my new life: 'So, what's new?'

'Delighted to see you looking so well, Mr Harris.'

I drop his hand. He's either near-sighted, joking, or a practiced liar.

'I wouldn't worry about the little dizzy spell Ms Caradet mentioned on the phone. It's a classic reaction in your condition. Did you drink any alcohol?'

I say no.

'Try not to until tonight, and by tomorrow it should be gone.'

He studies me in silence, smile fixed, like an artist admiring his work.

'So . . . what did you want to see me about?'

I lower my gaze, stare at an inkstain in the carpet.

'Is something bothering you? I'm here to listen to anything you might want to tell me, Mr Harris.'

His warm, mournful voice must push people to

confide in him. He looks like he gets so bored all alone. After listening to my silence for about ten seconds, he continues, as if he were answering me, 'On the other hand, it was good to try confronting external reality, even if it was a bit premature. We have you down as discharged but, while your brain is eliminating the excess of glutamate, I'd advise staying quietly at home for two or three days.'

'I no longer have a home.'

Barely a reaction. His nose dips toward the green leather blotter on which my chart is resting, the medical file of Martin Harris.

'What do you mean? When you got to your apartment, didn't you . . . find yourself at home?'

'That's just the problem. Can you help me?' I say in a burst of rancor.

'Some memory loss?'

'On the contrary, memory excess. Too much memory for two people.'

The friendlier he is, the more aggressive he makes me feel. He moves a paperweight and leans back.

'I'm listening.'

And so I describe my situation, once again. But this time, I tell it as if I really were a mythomaniac who's not fooled by any of it. And I add a few details, as if I resented him for bringing me back to life in someone else's skin.

He's stopped smiling. He stands up, skirts around his desk, and sits in the armchair next to mine. He lessens the distance between us: let's forget about doctor–patient and talk man to man. My fists are squeezed into a violence that I don't recognize.

'It does exist, Mr Harris.'

'What exists?'

'This kind of transfer. Let me be blunt,' he adds, even more serene than before. 'May I?'

He joins his fingertips in front of his nose, leaning on the left armrest, twisted around to face me.

'Perhaps you *believe* you're not an amnesiac. Amnesia doesn't always mean loss of memory. It's more complicated than that. It can also mean a refusal to pick up the thread.'

'What thread?'

He swallows, rubs the steel of his watchband.

'Comas are a fascinating *terra incognita*, about which we have only theoretical data, evaluations, scales. If I told you that you scored four out of eleven on the Glasgow Test, or I gave you the levels of your evoked potential, it wouldn't get you anywhere – or me either, now that you're awake. We feel our way around, we note, we classify, but we actually know almost nothing about it. Only what we hear from our patients. You're more or less the two hundredth that I've brought back to the surface – that I've welcomed, let's say. And I think I've encountered every kind of symptom you can imagine: confusion, prostration, exuberance, stories of being at death's door with the tunnel of light and angels, details of everything said around the bed, which the patient has heard perfectly, Korsakov's Syndrome, which erases painful memories, irreversible and reparable lesions, complete or partial loss of identity, immediate recoveries and others that take years . . .'

His eyes, now vague, look through me.

'One of my most interesting cases, only about six weeks ago, involved a young man who had perfectly recovered all his faculties, except one: social skills. When a visitor started to bore him, he said so. When someone smelled of sweat, he pointed it out. If someone was ugly, he remarked on it. He told his sincere feelings to each member of his family, which caused huge dramas. And it was impossible to make him understand that, socially, we're obliged to lie all the time. He found that absurd, unacceptable, even comical, as if someone were trying to make him recognize the moral necessity of urinating on people when you meet them. Not only had the imprint been erased, but a logic had filled the space.'

'But what's that got to do with me?'

'Before his coma, this young man had suffered greatly from self-censorship. Bullied in child-hood, religious boarding school, introverted character, repressed homosexuality, training to be a diplomat . . .'

'But again . . .'

'I'm trying to help you gauge the hidden and, as I said, *logical* work that can take place during the deep coma phase. We are coming to believe more and more that, in this phase, the brain is functioning at peak efficiency; it's just disconnected from its normal relations with the surrounding world. In your case, let's suppose for example that you're madly in love with a woman named Liz. You try to woo her, you follow her, you're obsessed with her and know nearly everything about her. But she's happily married and she tells you so with utter certainty and sincerity: she rejects you, leaving you no hope. On the contrary, she belittles you, devalues you by constantly invoking the castrating image of her husband. A husband who, moreover, is a brilliant man, socially desirable, physically superior . . . So at that point, what becomes the impossible dream of your life? To be him, in his place, married to this loving, emotionally fulfilled woman. Now comas can sometimes act as a kind of dream laboratory; they make possible, authentic, and attainable things that, under normal conditions, would be simple phantoms. Are you following me? Everything you've learned about this man, everything you've suspected, intuited, deduced, extrapolated, becomes *true*, becomes *you*. And when you wake up, you're convinced that you're him. And the undesirable one, your former self, is pushed back into your unconscious, incarcerated, destroyed.'

I've listened to him with arms folded, paralyzed.

'Yeah, but just hold on there . . . We're not talking about three or four bits of information I have in my head – it's an entire memory!'

He smiles, lowering his eyelids.

'That's normal: it's because of the glutamate. When the brain is deprived of oxygen, it releases massive quantities of this neuromediator, which plays a key role in memory generation: it's what favors synaptic transmission. Hence your illusion today of possessing the "entire memory" of the man onto whom you've transferred.'

'But you can't just invent a complete set of memories! Glutamate or not, I haven't transferred myself into this guy: I've lived his life! His whole life! Childhood, studies, professional experiences, losses, conjugal life . . . A thousand details, including the most obscure! How could I know all that?'

He takes a deep breath, stands up, and goes to the window, pulling aside the curtain to reveal a wall just outside.

'There, dear sir, we leave the field of the rational. All I can tell you is that there are examples, and I've met some of them myself, but I'm not supposed to say so in an establishment like this one. So I'm talking to you privately, letting you judge for yourself about phenomena that official medicine still deems utterly unacceptable.'

He turns around and leans his back against the library, his fingers squeezing a corner of the curtain. A ray of sunlight edges its way onto the floor, between the clouds.

'What are you getting at, doctor?'

'Let's say that the mind, to put together the elements of the fable it's building, will help itself.'

'Excuse me?'

'Our brains are composed of matter and energy, agreed? Of organic tissues and waves that don't necessarily interact in a closed system. What I'm trying to tell you . . .'

'Is that I cleaned out this guy's memory long distance.'

'Cleaned out? No, since you tell me that your memories are equal. More like scanned. The original is still in its place, but the copy is in you.'

I swallow, staring at the reflections playing over the window panes.

'Doctor, there's something I didn't tell you about. When I woke up, I had . . . It seemed like I had . . .'

He lets me wallow for a few moments in my ellipses before finishing my sentence: '. . . a near-death experience, is that it? You left your body,

86

you saw it from above, and you felt pulled into a tunnel by a great current of love and well-being. Then a luminous shape explained to you that it wasn't your time yet and you had to go back.'

I look at him, hands gripping the armrests.

'How did you know that?'

'Statistics. Thirty-five per cent of my patients report similar experiences. It's a simple chemical hallucination, brought on by lack of oxygen to the brain and the resulting discharge of glutamate. The overload of glutamate causes an excess of synaptic relays: too many doors open at the surface of the neurons, which we call NMDA receptors. Because of this, an overproduction of calcium invades the neuron and causes its death. The brain then has to manufacture urgently a substance to block the NMDA receptors – ketamine, a dissociative anesthetic that gives you the sensation of leaving your body, floating in the air, seeing shapes and lights. It's perfectly normal.'

His reassuring smile fills me with a mixture of rancor and disappointment. He uncaps his pen, furrows his brow, wipes the nib on the blotter. I recall my father's silhouette floating in the whiteness of the tunnel, the intense light that somehow wasn't blinding. My father in his gardener's uniform, restored to the time of his youth, magnificent and joyful, telling me gently, without moving his lips, *Don't be afraid, Martin. Go back to your body. You'll have a second existence. Only you can decide what to do with it.*

'The result is that, when you come to, the doping effects of the glutamate on your memory are all the stronger because the hallucinogenic ketamine has disconnected you from reality. The scenario you constructed for yourself in the coma thus has a power of truth greater than all the contradictory information you might be receiving now. So I'm not surprised that you refuse to accept the version I'm giving you.'

'But if you don't believe in near-death experiences, how can you believe in telepathy, brain waves hacking into other people's brains?'

'I don't believe in them. But I wanted you to tell me about your experience. Being able to verbalize the hallucination means you've made considerable progress, for a first session.'

His phone rings and he answers it, listens with brows knit.

'I'll be right there.'

He hangs up, preoccupied, tells me he's sorry but it's an emergency.

'So what happens now? Do I get put back to sleep for another brainwashing and wake up my old self?'

He slips his pen into his jacket pocket, changes his mind, and takes it out again to scribble something on his prescription pad.

'I don't see how an induced coma could change anything,' he murmurs while jotting. 'Are you free for dinner? I'd like to continue this conversation. I have a few more things to tell you that I can't decently mention inside these walls.'

He tears the slip from the pad and hands it to me.

'It's forty minutes from Paris. You can bring Ms Caradet, if you like.'

I glance at the address and fold the paper.

'Do you always invite your patients to the country?'

'Raking dead leaves is excellent therapy. No, seriously, you're an enigma to me, Mr Harris. When I come across a case that doesn't fit the usual profile, I either solve it or write about it.'

He points to the lower shelf of his library,

full of books with his name on the spines.

'In forty years of practice, I've never seen someone emerge from a coma with so much . . . immediate lucidity, self-possession, call it what you will. So much freshness, if you'll pardon my saying so. The explanation I gave you is just an academic hypothesis. But if you look at it with a little distance, if you analyze the share of fantasy that might factor into your current identity as you perceive it, in the light of this alter ego you've had contact with three times since this morning, then you might be able to reawaken the *other voice* inside you. The one you didn't want to hear anymore.'

'Doctor, tell me the truth. Am I crazy?'

He looks at me with a hint of a smile.

'I'll see you this evening. And try to wear boots, the ground is wet.'

He leaves without showing me out of his office. Maybe he thinks I'll see it as a mark of trust. Or he wants to leave me alone with his books so that I can become acquainted with them. I take one off the shelf, turn it over, skim through the brief bio and review quotes above his photo. Dr Jérôme Farge, *Who Must I Be?* Subtitle: *Neurophysiological Evaluation of Core Consciousness in Post-Comatose*

Identity Disorders. He doesn't seem like a quack, but nothing he said has struck a nerve. I feel like Martin Harris with every fiber in my body, with all my might, and even more so since trying not to be him. In all fairness, when I described my situation to the doctor, I tried to adopt the viewpoint of the ones who are out to negate me. But it didn't hold up. My internal reality is stronger – or my 'dream laboratory', as he put it. I smile at the idea of my brainwaves heading out to clone Liz's husband's. But try as I might to refute a theory that Dr Farge himself admits he doesn't believe in, I've spent too much time studying telepathy in plants to remain entirely deaf to the possibility. Except I'd take it in reverse: during my coma, for a reason I'm beginning to glimpse, I was the one who communicated the contents of my memory to Elizabeth's lover. The fact is, I was suffocating with her, since her depression; other women were starting to look better and better, but I swore to myself never to leave her, even if she wasn't the same anymore. It's true that I accepted this job in France to get us out of the dead-end of Greenwich, where she no longer saw anybody – and especially to get some breathing room outside our usual circles. The fact is, for months I kept having the same dream over and over again. I was looking at myself through the living-room window: I could see myself at home with Liz, and at the same time I was outside, doubled, free to go love other women without abandoning her, without leaving an empty space . . . But that makes no sense. If someone were to ask me what I want, what I really want since this morning, it would be to reclaim my place, chase out the intruder. However dissatisfied I might have been with Liz, I have too full a life just to give her up to some squatter. Who is apparently hanging onto my identity just as tenaciously.

The other possible explanation, of course, is the one voiced by my colleague at the INRA. Who else could have reason to discredit me, prevent me from pursuing my research, get me out of circulation – who else, if not the GMO producers that I'm attacking by endorsing Kermeur's work? That said, the stakes are high and they aren't suicidal: creating another me with false ID papers, even if they've bought my wife's complicity, can only work for a day or two – unless I were to disappear for good. After all, nothing says my accident couldn't have been attempted murder. Unless they're simply waiting for me to lose my mind in the face of this absurdity. To bang up against wall after wall until I go nuts, destroy myself like a moth against a lit window. To cut myself off from my milieu, alienate everyone's trust with my attitude, even Kermeur's – who will then choose, as he no doubt already has, to base his findings on the work of an impostor who'll lead him down the garden path, neutralize him with mistaken conclusions that will discredit him as well.

Still, there's a problem. I'm perfectly willing to believe Monsanto or someone else has the reasons and resources to put my life into someone else's head, but how could they know all these intimate details about me? Dad's snakes, his hot-dog contests . . . I've never mentioned those to anyone, not even Liz. Can we be indexed to such a point, from birth? And who controls the index files?

I grip onto the bookshelves, paralyzed by the idea that has suddenly hit me. And what if the psychiatrist were right? What if *I'm* the fake, the programmed replacement? If I'm the one who was to pass himself off as Martin Harris, and the coma just erased the memory of my imposture? I look for a mirror, my hands trembling, open a closet and look at myself in the full-length glass. The hypothesis is a dead end, I know, but just the fact of having envisioned it has changed something in me. You can't be thrown away by everybody without it leaving scars. You can't be flatly repudiated, delivered unto doubt and suspicion without it arousing a certain hardness, a streak of rage and hateful solitude. I've tried to convince them every way I know how: sincerity, reason, competence, emotion – all I have left is force. I'm in a state of self-defense, and I want the hide of the man who's taken my place. I want to see him dead. I can feel it. The woman from the INRA was right, before: the only logical outcome to our situation is to eliminate the extra one. I don't know what level of violence he's reached by now, but if he were standing here, in the mirror, in front of me, I would strangle him.

I shut the closet door, slip the book into the pocket of my raincoat, rediscover the twenty-euro bill. I'm sick of being all wrinkled, in these clothes that reek of silt and hospital. I want to change, but I barely have enough to buy a pair of socks. I look around for something that might be valu-able. Nothing apart from a statuette of Diana the huntress, bow taut on its bronze arrow: I can't quite see leaving the office with that under my arm. Delicately, I tear a dozen or so sheets from the prescription pad and slip them into my inside pocket before walking out.

Two orderlies chatting in the corridor nod at me as they cross my path. I answer with a cordial look. All the same, I think it's a bit negligent of them to leave a man like me at large.

6

I've lost everything, except my memory. He has stolen my wife, my job, and my name. I'm the only one who knows he isn't me. I'm living proof of that. But for how much longer? I'm in danger, sir. And you are my last hope.

A door opens; the secretary shows a client out. I gather my prepared phrases and stand up. She comes back into the waiting room and points me to the door, which she shuts behind me.

I was expecting a nosey little bugger with a hound's-tooth jacket and a shifty gaze, or a sweaty fat man with eyes swimming in bourbon: the stereotypes that go with the trade. But he's tall and bald, with a black polo shirt and boots and a body piercing.

'I don't do adultery cases,' he informs me right from the start. 'Only research into commercial, industrial, or inheritance information and verification of personal data.'

I confirm that I chose him with that in mind.

He motions toward the chair facing his desk. I add that it's the first time I've spoken to a private detective. He answers that the term is 'investigator'.

'What is this about?'

'Me.'

I'm about to launch into the call for help that I polished in the waiting room, but his aloofness and cold appearance push me toward sobriety.

'I'm an American citizen, I've lost my papers, and someone's taking advantage to try to steal my identity. Your ad says you have agents in the United States.'

'Correspondents, yes.'

'I need to prove who I am, urgently, to confound the impostor who is passing himself off as me.'

'Are you familiar with my fees?'

'No. It doesn't matter.'

'So, fill me in on the situation.'

I tell my story, one more time, with the annoying impression of detailing the other man's situation, of being a stranger to what's happening to me.

'Wouldn't you rather handle this with your consulate?'

'I've been there.'

'And?'

I summarize the results of my attempt: impossible to obtain a duplicate passport, personal records, fingerprint file, or even a certificate with just my social security number. I insisted, filled out twenty different forms, waited for three hours. I was finally seen by a guy in shirtsleeves who assured me that everything was under control: they have transmitted my requests to the relevant departments, only there was the usual delay in treating this kind of matter. When I asked what the usual delay was, he answered that it depended. But it was already the end of October and we shouldn't expect too much. Shaking my hand with a friendly air, he wished me good luck and said not to hesitate to call him if there was anything he could do, no matter what. I walked out of there, happy at first, and then I realized halfway down the stairs that I was leaving completely empty-handed: he hadn't even told me his name.

'So what is it you want me to do, exactly?' says the detective, kneading the diamond in the flare of his nose. 'To get your records faster than the American authorities? I don't want to give you false hope, Mr Harris. I'm expensive, but let's be realistic.'

'No, I was thinking that you could send your correspondents to check me out in Greenwich, where I lived, or at my campus. Ask my neighbors, my colleagues, show them my picture, take down their statements, get me supporting documents . . .'

'For whose benefit?'

His interrogation-like tone is getting on my nerves. I explain that I'm the victim of a plot by a multinational out to discredit my struggle against GMOs. Suddenly his face comes to life, his eyelids rise, and a glimmer of interest casts me in a new light.

'Monsanto?'

'Or its competitors.'

'If that's the case, you couldn't have picked anyone better: I'm in contact with the best law firm in Philadelphia, specializing in suits against industrial lobbies. I gave them the conclusive evidence in the Vivendi case . . .'

'No, thanks. I just want to prove that I'm me, that's all. I've prepared a list for you with the names of people and organizations to contact.'

He asks why I don't simply handle this myself.

'I no longer have a computer, or a phone, or a credit card. I reported the loss, but until I receive my new card . . .'

I immediately regret my confession of insolvency, which will no doubt cool his enthusiasm. But he's begun reading my two pages of names, addresses, references, biographical data, and his smile continues to widen. Obviously, the profit he hopes to gain from my case nicely exceeds the amount he could ask me for.

'You really managed to get plant testimony admitted in a court case?'

Respect has permeated his voice. I nod.

'I can understand why the GMO lobby is trying to break you,' he murmurs, standing up. 'I'll be right back.'

He goes out, taking with him those two sheets of paper that encapsulate a life. When earlier I dredged up the details from my memory to write them down, I felt the same nervousness as when I pack my suitcase, the same anxiety that I'm forgetting something essential. Every event was there for the asking, all the notable facts of my existence, but it was an effort to recall the images of the people and places I was evoking. My father in the garden of Disney World, my mother dressed up like a *vahine* delivering breakfasts down the hallways of the Polynesian Hotel, receiving my diploma at Yale, meeting Liz at a law-school party, our marriage with no family members present and only colleagues as guests, my first discoveries in the language of plants ... When I focused my attention, I felt like pieces of me were coming unstuck in my brain and moving to the background to compose a memory, recreate a scene. Each time it was the same feeling of tearing, ubiquity, dispersion. Like a tree losing its leaves, a flower disseminating its pollen. I've never experienced anything like it. I'm someone who has always built his life on a single note: rage, born of childhood humiliations. The feeling of injustice and rejection was transformed with the passing years into pride at being different, at standing apart from the human race and relying only on myself. I've always been collected, coherent, unassailable. Why did it feel like I was amputating a piece of myself every time I committed a memory to paper? Probably a side-effect of the coma – yet another one.

But there was this other, even stranger phenomenon, like a superimposition. As I was writing the date and place of my marriage, an image from somewhere else came to settle on top of the scene, blotting out the decor of the Greenwich Country Club. I'm with Liz on a street in Manhattan, precisely at the corner of Forty-second Street and Sixth Avenue, where the giant screen broadcasts live, every second, the sum total of the national debt and its amount per American household. I am kissing Liz, but I see myself from behind, from above, as when I floated over my body in the coma. And the liquid crystal numbers parade by, brighter and brighter, clearer and clearer: seventy-two billion, four hundred seventy million, seven hundred thirty-two thousand, eight hundred fifteen . . .

'Do you really want me to verify all these details? I would think that a statement from your university would be ample proof.'

The bald guy has come back in, and sets a photocopy of my life in front of me.

'Yes, every detail. I insist on having them all verified, so that I can prove it's *my* childhood, *my* career, *my* wife! That man has made away with my entire existence. I want us to be able to confound him point for point!'

He agrees zealously. It's crazy how quickly authority returns when you represent the promise of profit.

'I have to make a call. It's local.'

'Go ahead. Should I step out?'

'No need.'

He hands me the receiver and goes to open a file drawer. I call Muriel, tell her everything's fine and that Dr Farge has invited us to Rambouillet this evening. After three seconds of silence, she replies that she's delighted for me but that she can't make it: she has to help her son with his homework. But I can come for dinner at their place some other time. Her voice is toneless, impersonal. Without transition, she asks if I'm sure I'm feeling better. Overcoming my annoyance, I reply that she'll soon have definitive proof of my identity.

'Tomorrow at noon,' the detective specifies.

I glance up at him, impressed. He explains that time is money, and that we both lose by wasting it.

'As soon as he got my email, my correspondent answered that an operative was leaving for Yale and another one for Greenwich. If you wish, I'll order two more for Orlando and Brooklyn. Don't move.'

He presses the button on a digital camera, shows me the photo on the screen. At the other end of the line, I hear a man's voice giving Muriel an itinerary. I say goodbye and hang up, then ask the detective how long he was out of the room.

'Four or five minutes, I think . . . I worked as quickly as I could.'

Again that bizarre discontinuity in space and time the moment I search my memory; the impression that I've moved to the background for only ten seconds, and minutes have gone by without me.

'I'm transmitting your photo. Where can I reach you?'

'I'll call you. While we're at it, I also want to know the exact date when the gross national debt in America was at seventy-two billion, four hundred seventy million, seven hundred thirty-two thousand, eight hundred fifteen dollars.'

He jots it on a notepad. The good thing about a private eye is that nothing surprises him.

'Anything else, Mr Harris?'

'No.'

'Then I have one more thing: your mother. You didn't put down her address.'

'The last time I saw her I was thirteen. I've never forgiven her for what she did to my father.'

He marks a polite silence, halfway between discretion and indifference.

'But find her, if you can: it's the perfect opportunity. Ask at Disney World. She worked for room service at the Polynesian until 15 August 1975, when she ran off with a German banker. Günther Krossmann, room 3124.'

He notes it on his pad, smiling to himself.

'You've got some memory.'

'Thanks,' I say, standing up. 'See you tomorrow.'

Between the two mirrors in the elevator, I try to forget that cold anger, the rage that has gone undiminished since my first day without her, the dispassionate rancor I felt every time she called me to justify her actions, to accuse my father for the sudden passion she'd conceived for number 3124, and render me ultimately responsible for the abandonment that followed. She repeated over and over that the Bundesbank widower was the chance of a lifetime – and between the lines, that it made up for the rotten luck I incarnated: a one-night stand with a shabby nobody who hadn't pulled out in time. I had resisted the roller-coaster rides and purgative teas. I had clung on, and now that was my problem. She had put up with me and Dad for thirteen years. Now I was grown up and she was free. Being renounced by my wife today, as casually as I had been by my mother, is more than I can bear.

On the sidewalk, I find myself prey to an underlying violence that I don't know how to channel, a strength that I squeeze in my fists as the passersby skirt around me. No matter how often I repeat to myself that the truth is on the march, that the investigators will confirm my identity within hours, I can't quite become myself again. Feel like before. Without my realizing it, another personality has sprouted since this morning, that of the impostor they accuse me of being, and the paradoxical freedom that comes with it leaves me feeling less and less comfortable in my skin, unable to control what's happening to me. Like puberty that shocks the body, an energy that paralyzes you for as long as you don't dare use it, accept it, satisfy it.

I walk down Boulevard Sébastopol between

trees made fragile by the parking interdiction. I stop next to a condemned plane tree marked with a yellow cross. The salting of the roadsides every winter. Without the protection of parked cars along the curb, the traffic spews an acidic mix onto the tree trunks that will eat them away much more surely than dog urine. I hug the plane tree, to give it strength while absorbing some of its own – the exchange that punctuates my days. Nothing. I feel nothing. Not the vibrations of its sap in my veins, nor the dilation of the plexus, nor that kind of electric arc that courses through my body from hand to hand. I try again with its neighbor, then head into a small park to hug a younger, healthier linden, a centennial chestnut . . . Not the smallest echo, the slightest return signal. Even the trees don't recognize me anymore. Or else my nervous state perturbs them, acts as a screen, prevents me from receiving their signals. I absolutely must evacuate this tension.

I cross the boulevard and take a narrow street that leads me to the Forum des Halles. Earlier, when I came out of the subway, children were playing on the paving slabs, parents were frozen in place, and teenagers were breakdancing among the dead leaves. It is now six o'clock and night has just fallen. The families have returned home, the teens have taken their music and gone. In the rows of street lamps, between the shrubs and the bushes, dealers calmly greet their clients, take out samples, give tastes, negotiate, pocket the cash.

I choose a quiet spot between two troughs of forsythias, lean against a signpost, and wait.

7

A tiny convertible is double-parked in front of the Rambouillet train station. Perched on the fender, arms folded, Dr Farge sits in the rain. He watches me walk up and tells me I'm looking very dapper. I should: my suit cost six of his prescriptions. He shakes my hand, says he'll lend me some country clothes. I bend low to climb into his car. I feel no shame in his presence, no remorse. As if the fact that my identity is being denied has liberated me from every scruple, every value, every role society imposes on individuals to make them play their assigned part. I have no more limits, no more reference points, no more sanctions. Since no one recognizes me anymore. Since no one wants to know me anymore.

For a brief moment, as I was dealing in the Forum gardens, I told myself that I had to stop existing in order to start living. It wasn't me talking, but the voice wasn't unfamiliar to me, either.

'Do you find me different from before?'

He finishes backing up, puts the car in neutral, and looks me in the eye.

'Why? Should I?'

I'd forgotten that shrinks always answer a question with a question. I elude it with a motion toward the windshield: drive on. The acceleration throws me against the seat.

'It's the Honda roadster,' he comments. 'The only real extravagance I allow myself.'

The bumps in the road send my head banging against the roof. He hugs the bends, cruises over potholes at seventy miles an hour. Crushed against him, feeling like my ass is scraping the asphalt, I tell myself that you really shouldn't judge on appearances. I pictured him in a Volvo station wagon, with dual airbags and soft music. For his part, he surely takes me for a poor, honest slob.

'What are you thinking about?' he asks after a moment, as we're leaving town.

I repress a smile. I was thinking about my last customer, the standard black-kid-on-rollerblades, who had the nerve to lecture me about what I was doing. I retorted that, in any case, with or without my prescriptions, he'd have found a way to get his fix. As it was, I might even have saved the life of an innocent pharmacist. He chuckled on his rollers, gave me a slap on the shoulder, and told me I was cool. I'm especially good at handling myself in the jungle. Otherwise I never would have returned alive from my missions in the Amazon.

'If my questions bother you, just say so.'

'No, they're fine.'

We can barely make out the trees in the dim glow of the headlights. He turns on the AC, which freezes my face and thickens the fog on the windshield.

'Did you hurt yourself?'

'Just a bump.'

I fold down the vanity mirror to check the damage. Just a scratch on my cheekbone and the start of a bruise. A scooter ran me down as I was leaving the Forum, after shopping. I rolled on the ground. The helmeted passenger rushed at me, and then a whistle blast stopped him in his tracks. The two men vanished on their scooter. I thanked the cops, who had come out of nowhere and who warned me against walking around this neighborhood at this time of evening carrying Tendance D shopping bags.

'So what's new since this afternoon?' the

neuropsychiatrist asks in a jolly tone, wiping off the fog with his hand.

I keep mum about my transactions in the gardens of Les Halles, as well as about my shopping trip to sub-level 3 of the mall. I was scouting out the shops for a suit of the type I usually wear, an all-purpose outfit that doesn't wrinkle, when I stopped dead in front of Tendance D. The salesgirl was rearranging the display window. A brunette with long hair, petite, arched, breasts taut against raw silk, she was putting a shirt on a mannequin. The way she was dressing it was sexier than a striptease. She caught my gaze and smiled. The corridor was empty, apart from the cleaning crew dragging dry mops, the noise of metal shutters clanging down one by one. I went in.

'Are you closed?'

'That depends.'

She finished buttoning the shirt on the plastic man, tucked it into his pants, and straddled over the edge of the window. Her nipples stood out between two bats on the gore shirt knotted above her navel.

'Would you like to see something?'

She looked at my old blue herringbone jacket shrunken by the Seine. I nodded.

'You must be a good size 46.'

It sounded like a compliment. She added, riffling through her hangers, that this place didn't really seem my style. I answered that I no longer had a style: up to her to find me one. She immediately handed me an orange T-shirt and a vampire's frock coat, breathing in a warm voice, 'Try this on for me.'

She pulled aside the curtain of the changing room and I undressed without closing it. Desire was tying my throat in knots. The need to attract a stranger, to be looked at for my body, without the problem of who was occupying it. Hospital smells, that sour, chemical cleanliness, still permeated my skin – I wanted to bury them in the smells of fucking, to drown Liz's betrayal in the body of another. And this desire was enough for me. It wasn't a fantasy, but a rehabilitation – as you might say about an abandoned building that you're trying to restore.

Bare-chested in the changing-room mirror, I looked like what I am: a man of the forests disguised as a product of civilization, shaved, combed, creamed, pasteurized: a woodsman from the city. The equivalent of a ski instructor away from the slopes – no charm, no interest, no color once out of his element. Still, the girl stole glances at me as I flexed my muscles while slipping on the T-shirt. I could tell she liked me. Even if her only goal was a sale.

'Maybe something like this instead,' she concluded, showing me the outfit I'm wearing now.

Standing in front of her, I put on the hip-huggers, the collarless shirt, the jacket with its eight buttons. I looked like a clergyman in bell-bottoms. With her arms folded, she watched me get a hard-on under the snug-fitting trousers and confirmed that they were the right size.

'Can you do the hems while I wait?'

She knelt down to stick her pins in me.

'It's just a two-liter, but it has great pick-up.'

I imagine he's talking about his engine. I nod, erase the salesgirl's mouth from my eyes.

'And what about you – what do you drive back in the States?'

'I've got a Ford.'

'How many cylinders?'

'I don't really know. It's got a big trunk.'

Silence. He slows down, stops in front of a rusty gate. His fingers resting on the door handle, he probes for more information. 'Do you play chess?'

'No.'

He gets out to open the creaky gates, gets back in to tell me that the weatherman promises it'll clear by tomorrow, and asks me what I think. I answer that it's possible, if that's what they said. He points out that, after an experience of imminent death, people often have premonitions. I answer that it's not the case with me.

He continues on to the end of a long driveway, parks on a gravel surface. The house is an old cottage squeezed between a cluster of rhodo-dendrons and a huge magnolia lying on its side. I get out and approach the tree.

'The Christmas '99 storm,' he comments sadly. 'I didn't want to cut it down. And now more than ever . . . The landscaper didn't give it much hope, but see for yourself: it's surviving. Aside from my patients, I don't listen to anyone.'

I tell him I agree, so as not to put a damper on his evening. Trees always flower more before dying, to ensure their lineage.

'You have an enviable profession, Martin. Tell

me, honestly, can you really communicate with trees? Do they talk to you?'

'Very clearly.'

'How so?'

'It depends on the species.'

'I envy you. Humans can be so repetitive.'

'I can keep quiet.'

'I didn't mean you. Go on in, it's open. My housekeeper's here. I'm going to fetch some wood and I'll be right back.'

I open the door with its little glass panes, and am immediately enveloped by the smell of beef stew and fresh wax. A brutal sadness grips me in the gut. The interior of this single man's home is a hundred times warmer than our home in Greenwich, which never smelled of food or basic household activities, but gave off only the artificial aroma of potpourri in bowls. The kitchen is tidy, decorated with useful objects, polished, alive. A vacuum cleaner shuts off; an old woman comes in to say hello and tells me there are slippers in the basket. I follow her into the living room with its low exposed beams. She makes me sit in a sunken couch, between a piano covered with a tablecloth and the fireplace in which kindling is stacked over balls of newspaper.

'Mineral water or fruit juice?'

I smile in spite of myself. Here, apparently, guests don't mix alcohol and antidepressants.

'There's champagne in the icebox,' the doctor calls out, walking in with a basket full of logs. 'Thank you, Bernadette.'

Bernadette turns with a grunt and heads back into the kitchen.

'It's nothing against you, it's for my ulcer. Would you like to see your room?'

I tell him I hadn't planned to spend the night.

'Is someone expecting you?'

I let him light the fire without answering. He coughs from the smoke and opens the window a crack.

'Make yourself at home, Martin.'

I watch him distrustfully, in his woolen shirt and canvas pants. I don't believe in pure generosity: you only help those who can help you. I read through his *Who Must I Be?* on the train. If he's trying to understand my case, it's to get inspiration, draw conclusions, support his thesis. He brought me here to get raw material for a book in progress, in which I'll be designated by a single initial. Another way of negating my identity.

'Well, I'll be going,' says Bernadette at the kitchen door, removing her apron. 'Careful not to burn the stew. I put it on low. And don't forget to take the ice-cream sandwiches out of the freezer before you toss the salad.'

Two minutes later, backfire from a motorbike mixes with the crackling of the burning twigs. Dr Farge delicately lays an oak log across the andirons, replaces the fire screen, then goes into the kitchen. I hear the refrigerator being opened, glasses clinking, peanuts falling into a dish. A large black dog comes up silently to place a paw on my foot and look me over. I say hello; he doesn't move. I stretch out a hand to pet him but he backs away and goes to lie down in front of the piano, watching me the whole time.

'His name is Troy. He's a Beauceron,' the doctor says, coming back in with a tray.

'He seems nice.'

'He never barks. He attacks and kills. He's not my type, but he was a gift from Bernadette. The last of the litter. I couldn't refuse. Since then, we don't see any burglars around here. Nor the mailman, for that matter.'

He tips the bottle and opens it by turning it

around the cork. With meticulous precision he pours our drinks, carefully dosing the foam, aligning the levels of both glasses. Then he sits facing me on the couch, lets himself be absorbed by the velvet cushions, empties his glass, and leans forward, elbows resting on his knees.

'So. Now that we're away from the hospital, I can tell you privately what I couldn't say earlier. If you want me to, that is.'

I invite him to continue with a vague gesture.

'Have you made any progress since this morning? What I mean is, do you still believe you *really are* Martin Harris?'

'Yes. And it has nothing to do with glutamate.'

'Do you have any further proof to back you up?'

'I'm expecting some.'

A jet flies over the house at low altitude, with a sharp whine of engines. With pursed lips, he lets the silence fall again, then looks at his watch.

'It's 3.30 p.m. back home. If you'd like to call someone, please feel free.'

'I've hired a detective to contact my acquaintances.'

He ratifies my choice by spreading his hands. I

thought he would insist. Faces, names, numbers parade through my brain. My assistant Rodney; the dean of my department; Mrs Fowlett, who's watching our house; the Browns, who kept inviting us to dinner ... I have no desire to call any-one I know, without being able to tell if this is from embarrassment or apprehension. I refuse to demean myself by seeking corroboration from the upstart who's eyeing my salary, or the old pedant who's trying to dissuade me from impli-cating the university in my attacks on GMOs, or Ms Temperamental, who thinks she runs the place because she's the only one who can work the alarm, or the neighbors, who I have to beg not to keep pruning their hundred-year-old catalpa. But there's something else to my reticence: the fear of getting a reaction like the one I got from Liz. It's impossible, and I know it, but it's stronger than I am. And in any case, over the phone they could easily mistake my voice for the impostor's. Even if they authenticated me, it wouldn't prove a thing. Better to let the investigators show them my photo.

Another jet flies overhead, louder than the first. Jérôme Farge abruptly reaches for a remote control, points it at the stairway. An operatic voice fills the room, vocalizes over a percussive background. He shuts it off after a minute.

'My apologies,' he says. 'They opened a flight path in July, just above us. Since then I've spent my evenings counting Airbuses and blaring Wagner and Pavarotti to try to drown them out. No more Chopin – he's no match for the jets.'

This is the second time I've glimpsed the human being piercing through the man of science. His boyish pleasure at driving a young man's sports car, and this stubborn nostalgia that sentences his piano to silence.

'Do you play?' he asks.

He has followed my gaze toward the Pleyel. I answer with a pout that could express incompetence just as easily as modesty. I don't remember myself sitting at a keyboard, and yet a prickling in my veins, a slight impatience in my fingertips, is drawing me toward the instrument.

'Go ahead,' he encourages. 'My wife was the one who played, but I keep it in tune.'

I sit on the bench, intrigued by this internal call that corresponds to neither a memory nor a feeling of lack. I fold back the tablecloth, rest my good hand in the middle of the keyboard. I wait. I'm searching for a reflex, an autonomous movement, and end up clearing my brain by letting my fingers wander. At the first chords of the melody, I shut the fallboard.

'You haven't forgotten,' he declares in admiration.

'Yes, I have.'

I return to my chair near the fire. He asks if it's Gershwin. I have no idea. I answer that I've gotten rusty, so he'll leave it alone. He doesn't insist. My gaze lost in the flames, I vainly scan the house in Greenwich, the one where I was born, the cousin's apartment in Brooklyn, my dorm at Yale . . . No trace of a piano anywhere, no image of me learning music or practicing scales. It's not in my history. It's not a memory of mine. And yet, I know how to play.

He refills our glasses, offers me the dish of peanuts, sets it back on his knees. I can't tell if he's noticed my confusion or not.

'Do you believe in reincarnation, doctor?'

'What, like the notion of previous lives? The idea that all the infants born into the world are recycled corpses? The theory that if you've behaved badly, you'll pay for it in the next life by being born unlucky, unhealthy, and poor? No. That's just auto-suggestion and it doesn't get you anywhere.'

'Two-thirds of the planet believes in it.'

'Two-thirds of the planet is also starving, but that doesn't justify famine. That said, if you're asking me specifically in relation to your coma, my answer wouldn't be so unequivocal.'

A shiver runs up my spine.

'Why?'

He leans forward, raises a cushion behind him, and falls back again.

'I'm going to tell you about a case I was consulted on which was even stranger than yours. One evening last year, a young woman in Deux-Sèvres held a séance with some friends, just for fun. Sitting around a table, they made a glass spin, with the illusion that the deceased was answering their questions. Yes, no, banalities, contradictions . . . At the end of the seance, they turned the lights back on and blew out the candle. The young woman looked odd. They asked if she was okay, and she answered in Spanish. Her husband was surprised – he never knew she spoke that language. But the more they asked her, the more she answered in Spanish. No one else there spoke it, and they begged her to stop kidding around, but to no avail. It was as if she no longer understood French. The joke wasn't funny anymore, tempers rose, their friends went home, and her husband went to bed in a huff. The next morning at breakfast, he found her speaking Spanish to their children and holding them tight. He began to get seriously worried and went to fetch the concierge, who translated what his wife was saying: that her name was Rosita Lopez, that she had died the week before in Barcelona, that she had no intention of leaving earth and was perfectly comfortable in this family. They called the town doctor, who diagnosed a split personality. And they checked out her story. It turned out that a certain Rosita Lopez had in fact passed away eight days earlier in Barcelona.'

He downs a handful of peanuts and I watch him chew. He pours us more champagne before continuing.

'They took her to see a dozen specialists, including me. We noted the change of language, but medically we couldn't detect any schizophrenic symptoms, any ambivalence, none of the syndromes you normally see in cases of multiple personality. The patient was perfectly coherent, perfectly settled; her mood was stable, her obsessions permanent: she adored her children and desired her husband, who did his best to resist the passions of this stranger who was sharing his life. And then one day, unable to stand it anymore, he went to see an exorcist, who through prayers and imprecations finally managed to expel the intruding spirit. With that, the young woman recovered her identity and went back to being what she was before, with one difference: she still spoke Spanish. The infestation was so strong that it had contaminated the language area, in the left side of her brain. The poor thing had to learn her native tongue all over again.'

I stare at the bubbles rising in my glass. If he's drawing a parallel with my story, I'll ask him which side he puts me on: infested or infester.

'Do you know,' he resumes, 'that laboratory mice continue to find their way in a maze even after 90 per cent of their brain has been removed?'

'What's that got to do with me?'

'And that Dr McDougall at Harvard proved that other mice, bearing no biological relationship to the ones that had memorized the path, managed, years later, to find the exit just as quickly? As if the maze itself contained the memory of past experiences . . . The question I'm trying to lead you to, Mr Harris, is, where is memory stored? In our brains, or outside of us? Why, when we electrically stimulate a precise spot of the hippocampus several times over in a single patient, does it immediately revive an important memory, but *never the same one*? Could our brains be not so much a warehouse as a receiver? I'll go even further. How can a brain deprived of oxygen, fully dysfunctional, in a comatose state, store and process long-term memories, as is the case in near-death experiences? Because on the point of death, as probably during a mediumistic trance, the right temporal lobe is abruptly activated, connected in spite of itself to a database located outside the body. *Your* database . . . or that of a wandering soul, or of the man whose wife you covet.'

I set my glass down, push away the dish he holds out to me.

'Why do you always tell the story from that side? Why couldn't it be the other guy who bootlegged *my* database?'

'Because his wife recognizes him.'

An old-fashioned telephone jingles on a side table. Farge pries himself from the cushions and answers it in a doleful voice. His face immediately brightens.

'Yes, everything's fine. I'll put him on. My best to your family.'

He sets the antique appliance with its spiraling cord on my knees. Muriel apologizes for earlier: she had just taken on a fare and couldn't talk. She's sorry not to be joining us for dinner. She asks how it's coming along. I explain that Monsanto and cohorts have set up the entire thing, I'm certain of it and I'll have the proof tomorrow.

'Enough Nintendo!' she shouts. 'I said go to bed, do you see what time it is? Go tell your sister to turn down that music, I'm on the phone! Are you still there, Martin?'

The tenderness in her voice constricts my throat. It's not tenderness, moreover, but disarray. The honesty of letting me hear that she feels alone in the middle of her brood and that, perhaps, she misses me.

'So, everything's okay otherwise? Stew and ice-cream sandwiches?'

'All fine.'

'A word of advice: watch out for the burgundy. Well, have a good rest of the evening.'

'Muriel . . . The next time we see each other, my problem will be solved. But I'm happy about one thing: it gave me a chance to know you.'

It rings false, and yet I meant it sincerely. She answers that it's nice of me to say so. Modesty or politeness. The doctor stirs the embers, tactfully ignoring us. Muriel cuts the conversation short, asks me to let her know when I find anything out, adds lots of love. Once more her voice sounds hollow, like those translators on television who neutrally say 'I' in place of someone else. I hang up with a strange feeling, a mix of regret and spite. My head is heavy with all the things I should have said.

'She's a courageous woman,' the doctor states, believing he's echoing my thoughts.

I wrinkle my nose, tell him something's burning. He lets go of his poker, runs to the kitchen, lets out a curse, and drops the pot. I go in to help him mop up the stew.

'No matter, I'll make us an omelet. Don't worry about it, go back and relax.'

I open the door and walk out into the garden. The rain has stopped. I take a few steps into the acrid smell of wet lawn. Lights go on all around me. The setting is marvelous, ghostly, peaceful. Boulders, tiered gardens that bloom in sequence, the last roses of the season surrounded by Japanese chrysanthemums and winter jasmine.

I go from one tree to another, put my arms around them. They welcome me. *These* trees I can feel – not like the ones on Boulevard Sébastopol. Or else it's I who have changed since before. It's I who have again become receptive, identifiable. What restored the communication? That worried confidence and supplication I sensed in Muriel's voice, or the fact of having taken control of the situation at the Forum des Halles? Once again I feel in harmony with my immobile brothers. I feel united with their frequencies; my blood pulses to the rhythm of their sap. The energy we exchange dissipates anxieties, doubts, the unease of the city. Even as a child, I never really felt settled unless I was touching tree bark. A week away from the forest and already I became a different person. I rest my plexus against a willow, my back against a purple beech; I fondle the oaks and talk to the surviving plum trees in the tangle of the orchard. But the reunion is spoiled by a question that nags at my brain: why did the piano seem as familiar to me as these trees?

Jérôme Farge joins me, hands in his pockets among the dead apple trees, and says that he can't quite make up his mind to dig them up – they're such a part of the landscape. I tell him he's right: the pleurotus that grows on rotting wood eats nematode worms and prevents them from attacking living roots. With its sticky filaments, the mushroom forms a kind of lasso that smothers its prey by making its cells swell up. Without the parasites on their dead neighbors, his plum trees wouldn't be doing nearly so well.

He nods his head and murmurs, 'You really are a botanist.'

'Of course I'm a botanist!'

'What I mean is . . . You're definitely a colleague of Martin Harris, there's no doubt about it.'

I grab him by the shoulders and spin him around to face me.

'Listen, doctor. That man has false papers, my wife's complicity, and a mission to discredit me with the INRA in my battle against GMOs. Got it? I'm even starting to think that my accident was really an attempted murder. My replacement couldn't have been improvised in six days. Everything was planned before I even arrived in France, they followed me from the airport, and when they saw their chance . . .'

'I don't mean to discourage you, but paranoia is also a side effect of glutamate.'

'You can go to hell with your glutamate!'

The dog rushes up, stops one yard away from me, and stares at me with teeth bared.

'Smile,' says Jérôme Farge, tapping my shoulder. 'Look relaxed, like me. Everything's fine, Troy, he's a friend, we're just playing. Sit.'

The Beauceron slowly stretches out on the ground, not taking his eyes off me.

'If I needle you, Martin, you know it's only to test you. To gauge your degree of certainty. See if you really believe all the things you're telling me.'

'And what about you? What do you believe?'

Looking me squarely in the eye, he answers, 'I believe in your humanity. You're a good person, I'm certain of that.'

'Yeah, and what do you know about it? I stole

some of your prescription slips and I sold them to buy this get-up!'

I've blurted out the confession without understanding this burst of aggression, this need to kick him for his kindness. But he keeps smiling. And not only for the dog's sake. He says it's funny, but Muriel's daughter pulled the same trick on him two years ago, when he was treating her after her suicide attempt. She had prescribed herself amphetamines, which she came to show him as a provocation, to prove she wasn't as 'out of the woods' as he claimed, that she was free to start up again whenever she felt like it. He told her to keep them as a gauge of trust, a risk for which he would accept the consequences. She mailed them to him the following summer, along with a photocopy of her hairdressing certificate and a snapshot of her boyfriend.

'Just out of curiosity, how much does one of those things go for?'

'One hundred fifty euros.'

He remarks, with some bitterness, that it's more than an office visit.

The dull noise of an airliner envelops us; the lights on its wings blink among the willow branches, disappear behind the thatched roof.

'Once,' he sighs, 'you couldn't hear a sound here. A real sanctuary. I savored the absence of noise the way you savor a cognac, the glass cupped in your hands. It's gone forever.'

His sadness mollifies me. For the first time, I don't feel under scrutiny. The dog gets up and lopes away, goes to lie down in its kennel. I look for something comforting to say.

'In any case, your garden is very well maintained.'

'For who? And for how long? My son teaches in Tahiti. He'll sell the house when I die. I'll end up haunting the idiotic couple who've had their eye on it for ages,' he adds, indicating the huge villa behind the oak trees. 'The kind that expands from year to year, the model family who keep hatching kids one after another and get together on the weekends. In the winter, they use a motorized leaf-blower as if it were a rake, and the rest of the time they shave their thousand square yards with a mulching mower. If they got their hands on this place, they'd rip out all the trees and dynamite the rocks so they could mow it flatter. Their idea of a garden is a golf course.'

He turns back toward his house, head lowered. I follow him inside.

'Are you hungry?' he asks, heading once more into the kitchen, with a distraught look at the empty frying pan on the stove.

'No. The peanuts are fine.'

'I've got pretzels, too. And some black olives.'

He takes a bottle of burgundy and a corkscrew from the buffet and we go back to collapse into the soft cushions near the fire.

'When my wife was alive, it was heaven here. At least, I never noticed the nuisances. How is it?' he asks, seeing me taste the wine.

'Perfect,' I say, so as not to make him even sadder.

'For the past five years, I've been living with cancer in remission. I'm tired of dealing with it on my own, but I believe I'm still useful to too many patients to give up. I've had some successes, I've published the books I wanted, lived for thirty years with a happy woman. I've got no complaints. I'm finishing off my burgundy and my firewood. I've still got thirty-six bottles of Nuits Saint Georges 1970 and two-thirds of the oak tree that died the same year as my wife. It's already dry enough for the fireplace, but the wine is starting to turn, don't you think?'

I admit it.

'I thought so, from the color. I've lost my sense of taste since I've been alone. Psychosomatic ageusia – the only case I've ever encountered, and it's me. But I still get pleasure from seeing – colors and memories . . .'

The crackling of the logs melts into the fading sound of jet engines, covered over by a nearer rumbling.

'Martin.'

'Hmm?'

'Go on up to bed if you're tired.'

I sit up, head in a fog, the taste of smoke in my mouth.

'Have I been asleep? How long?'

'Three Airbuses. Long enough for me to add a log and pour myself another glass.'

'I'm sorry . . .'

'Please, no need. Boring people when I talk probably helped me decide to become a psychiatrist.'

The wine swirls before his eyes in the glow of the flames. He resumes after a moment.

'Your sleep is instructive.'

'Did I say something?'

'You called out. Three times.'

'Liz?'

'Would you like to talk about her?'

I stretch, empty my glass, swallow a handful of olives.

'What's the use? I don't even know who my wife is anymore. I don't know how long she's been with the other side.'

'I don't believe in this idea of a plot against you. Let's come back to your near-death experience for a moment, shall we?'

'You don't believe in those, either.'

'We were at the hospital. If I didn't show some skepticism, they would have slashed my departmental budget a long time ago.'

He gets up to replace the log that has rolled under the andirons. He sets down his tongs and turns around. His back against the fireplace, he ponders me for a moment while lighting a cigarette, holds out the pack. I tell him I don't smoke anymore.

'Since when?'

'It was Liz who quit.'

I see us sharing a cigar, early in our love, passing it to each other every two or three puffs, at a table, isolated in a cloud of smoke, glad to shock the other diners and create a void around us . . .

He sits back down.

'Last June, a patient emerged from a Glasgow 4 coma, like you, but completely amnesiac. Every time I asked her a question, she answered, 'There's a torn sneaker on the cornice.' And she pointed to the ceiling. To the point where I finally asked someone to go check. They found the shoe, two floors up, just as she had described it, but placed in such a way that it wasn't visible from any window in the hospital, nor from the ground, nor from the roof – only if you climbed a ladder leaning against the building. Or if you were float ing above the street.'

I hold my breath. A weight in my chest has lifted with every one of his sentences. A wave of lightness glides along the back of my neck.

'When you thought you were leaving your body, what was your emotional state?'

I close my eyes, trying to recapture the feelings.

'I wasn't afraid. More like surprised and confident. But it all seemed to go by so fast . . .'

'What were you thinking of?'

'Liz. I wanted to tell her what had happened to me.'

'Your accident or your death?'

'The accident. I never felt like I was dead.'

'Were you back with her?'

'I think so. After that came the tunnel of light, and my father telling me . . .'

'Never mind the tunnel. I'm interested in Liz. Were you at home, in your room?'

'I'm not sure. When I try to recreate the surroundings, I see another image instead. A different day. We're on a street in Manhattan and we're kissing. I see us from above, as if I were hovering over us.'

'Dissociated? You see your *living* body, in a moment from the past . . .'

'Possibly. But I don't remember ever having kissed Liz in that place.'

'Where is it, exactly?'

'At the corner of Forty-second Street and Sixth Avenue, beneath the ticker-tape that displays the national debt, with the portion per American family.'

'Which was how much?'

'Sixty-six thousand two hundred nine dollars,' I say automatically.

'Your memory is incredibly precise.'

I open my eyes.

'For that kind of asinine detail, yes. But I have no recollection of that kiss in real life.'

'It's a symbolic image.'

'It's always in my head.'

'And the number is always the same?'

'Always. And always from the same perspective.'

'So it's a recurrent dream, but it's identical every time.'

'No, not every time. When I fell asleep just now, I found myself back at the same scene. Except that Liz pulled away ... and I saw my face. It wasn't me.'

'That's logical: your dream is incorporating your current situation.'

'But it wasn't the other man either! I don't know who this one was, I've never seen him before.'

He sighs and falls backward, crosses his legs.

'The root of your problem really seems to be jealousy.'

'I've never been jealous! Before my accident, I never suspected Liz of seeing other men. And I wouldn't have minded if she had – quite the opposite!'

He raises his hand so that I'll let him finish.

'You're in a deep coma, with electrical activity in the cortex independent of any surrounding stimulus, agreed? Your disconnected consciousness – let's call it your 'astral body' – transfers itself into Liz's bedroom, and let's say for argument's sake that you find her making love to the other man. You can't bear the sight, despite what you say, so in your dream you replace it with the screen-image of a simple kiss shared with a stranger in the street. But at that moment, in the room, the double effect of jealousy and your refusal to die results in your astral body taking over the personality of her lover. With the same determination that we witnessed in Rosita Lopez. Except that, after this, a life instinct, perhaps triggered by your refusal to *give up your place*, brings you out of the coma, in full possession of your faculties. But the impregnation remains in the lover's memory on which you've trespassed. And so we have a kind of mental ubiquity, the fact that now two Martin Harrises coexist – one just as sincere as the other, from what you tell me.'

He pauses to let me absorb all this.

'What I can't explain is why your wife chose the infested one and erased you from her memory.'

I put my glass down. That last part I *can* understand.

'This is all just speculation, of course,' he says, stifling a yawn. 'Let it sink in, we'll talk about it more tomorrow.'

I stand up. He takes me to my room, wishes me goodnight, then turns around at the door. And he murmurs in a completely different voice, with disarming gentleness, 'That was the first time I've heard the piano since . . .'

He walks away down the hall, head low.

I close the door, get undressed, slip beneath the embroidered sheets that smell of mint and cinnamon. Two initials are intertwined: J and V.

I, too, had loved Liz, passionately. So why do I feel so removed from her, not even angry with her anymore? Why, when I turn off the light, does her face blend with Muriel's, her body with the image of the salesgirl at the Forum? Why do unknown women come into my head with every passing airplane? And why do I feel so comfortable tonight, all alone, my limbs spread out in this double bed?

8

She opens the shutters and leans out toward the
street. She stretches out her hand to see if it's
raining. She is wearing one of my shirts, as she
always does when she gets up. She disappears,
leaving the window open.

I pull back into the doorway where I've been
freezing for the past hour. She always slept naked,
and put on my shirt from the day before to go
make breakfast. The only ritual from our early days
to withstand the passage of time. My stomach
tightens at the memory of the coffee aroma that
rose every morning to infiltrate my dreams. I
would go join her in the kitchen and we'd make
love one day out of two, depending on what was
on the talk show she was watching distractedly,
from room to room, on the three television sets
that were permanently left running. Unless the
interest of the topic or the celebrity of that
day's guest kept her on the living-room couch in
front of the giant screen, tray on her knees, in

which case I took my coffee into the bathroom.

This morning, I had only decaffeinated green tea and soy crackers. The neuropsychiatrist's breakfast. He was still asleep; the housekeeper was ironing underpants next to my bowl. She told me I looked better than last night. I answered that her stew was delicious.

'Why, did the dog tell you?'

I blushed in the heat of the iron. She shrugged her shoulders, grumbled that with the doctor she was used to cooking for nothing: he ate like a bird. She was heading to the market in Rambouillet and asked what I'd like for breakfast. I asked her to drop me at the station instead. The doctor had helped me, less with his theories about my coma than with his own situation, his confidences, his resigned distress and active impotence. I left him a thank-you note on the table. In the garden that was dripping in the sunlight, Bernadette called to the dog, in vain.

'The Doberman next door's in heat again,' she groused, pulling down the roadster's convertible top.

She drove like a real myopic, constantly adjusting her steering, crossing over the white line and speeding up on turns, provoking honks and headlight signals from the cars we met. She yelled above the roar of the engine, in the howling wind: 'My old man and I used to do road rallies when we were young. I was the one who taught the doctor how to drive.'

A blue station wagon had been following us since we entered the forest. Suddenly it passed us in the middle of a bend, cutting us off. Bernadette's sudden yank of the wheel almost sent us into the ditch. She railed for a good five minutes against the village cops, who according to her were blotto by dawn. I didn't say anything, but that wasn't a police car.

Paranoia took hold of me again in the train to Paris. I felt watched from behind the newspapers, changed carriages at every station. Again I saw the yellow truck bearing down on Muriel Caradet's taxi, the motorbike rushing toward me at the Forum des Halles . . .

Liz reappears in the window, shakes out a tablecloth. The crumbs slide along the tiled slope and fall into the gutter. She pauses a moment to take in the view. She seems much more relaxed than in Greenwich. I don't know what she did with her time back then. She told me golf, classes, bridge at the country club, charity work at the church, but in the evening, coming home from the university, I would find her in the same place on the couch, with a glass of scotch and the news on CNN. Judging by the mileage on her car, if she went out at all, it was on foot.

She shuts the window. I try to recall the apartment, to visualize the rooms that I know only through photos that Kermeur emailed me. The living room with its sloped ceiling overlooking Faubourg-Saint-Honoré, the large kitchen looking out on the courtyard, and the bedroom in front of which I'm keeping watch, on Rue de Duras . . . An old-money, bijou kind of place, with dolls everywhere: the interior of an old woman's house. I wonder how much Liz has transformed it in a week, she who turned my wood-shingled house into a model of New England chic.

I remember our last Monday in Greenwich, in the silence of the woods already reddening with autumn, those woods that oppress her in winter and give her allergies in the spring. Another one of those mornings when I went to work, leaving her to rot her brain with a fistful of health bars and Jenny Jones. The ecstatic hostess was promenading her microphone among a bunch of clairvoyants so they could give the audience news of their dear departed, between two commercials in which lawyers vaunted their success against malpracticing doctors. The star that day was an over-inflated bimbo who communicated with animals, acting as interpreter between a Labrador and its master. Liz loved it. She believes in all this. She jotted down the addresses of the mediums, including the dog translator, even though we don't have any pets. I reproached her for her gullibility. She retorted that I should talk, with my trees. I got annoyed, said that had nothing to do with it, that what bothered me wasn't the phenomenon itself but the exploitation of suffering nincompoops, and we yelled at each other against a background of soliciting lawyers. She called me a schizo, I slapped her, and she fell back, smacking her forehead against the base of the lamp.

I raise my eyes. My replacement is leaning against the window guardrail, with the face of someone who has slept in. He's smoking, detached, calm, in my Hermès pajamas from Kennedy Airport. She hands him a cup, which he takes without a look, automatically. As if he has known this life as long as I have.

A mother and two little girls dressed for tennis turn the corner. The two girls tell each other secrets behind their rackets, throw a glance my way, and go back to their confidences, their hidden laughs. Their mother hurries them on, opens the back door of the car, shoves them inside by pushing their heads, like the police when they're arresting someone. Liz wanted a child. As for me, I don't know. I don't know anymore. I suffered too much from my father's shipwreck to want to be called Daddy. I would have liked to teach a little boy about trees, that's all. But I couldn't have stood it if he didn't care, listened distractedly while chewing gum before turning back to his video game.

It's amazing how much I continue to have thoughts from *before*, pathetic moments of nostalgia, remorse over my behavior that outweighs my grievances as a victim. The harm I did to Liz is minor compared to what she's putting me through now, but it doesn't change what I feel. Even if there's nothing left between us, everything I once felt for her remains intact, incredibly new. It's strange how the fact of being excluded from the present can reinvigorate the past.

They've gone back inside, shut the window, and from far away I hear the muffled sound of a piano. It might be him. If he knows as much as I do about botany, then logically he's also a pianist. But why would that aspect of his personality have leached into me, and only that one? Why, if our memories have fused, don't I have any other recollections that come from him?

I jump. An orchestra has just joined in with the piano. It's a recording. That doesn't prove or resolve anything, but I smile all the same, as if I've scored a point against the absurdity I'm battling. In my position, how can I define what is realistic and what isn't? No matter how much I keep turning over Dr Farge's hypothesis about my 'mental ubiquity', the way my consciousness at the point of death grafted itself onto the brain of my rival, the infestation that made him my duplicate, I still don't believe it. But I have no arguments to support my doubts. Other than the very personal feeling that, if you took away my memories, there would be nothing of me left in him.

The smell of burnt fat wafts from the exhaust

vent above my head. It's eleven o'clock and the restaurant kitchens are firing up. The bittersweet odor brings back my years of fast food on Coney Island, under my Nathan's hat. Again I see myself getting out of school, the ten elevated subway stops between John Dewey High School and Surf Avenue, the white building with its terrace roof parading golden letters under a smiling sausage, in the shadow of the abandoned Figure 8: *More than just the best hot-dog*. And that odor that permeated my hair and resisted every shampoo, the odor of my nights at the grill that made the girls in high school wrinkle their noses, that odor that would one day pay my college tuition and that, at the time, prevented me from going out.

I know why the other man is a fake. You can see it in his face, his ease, his detachment. He has never known shame, has never sought out the contempt in a girl's eyes. He never stank of French fries. I know full well that this argument is no match for the proofs I'm expecting about my identity, but it's the one that resonates most deeply in me. The lack of shame. And I believe I feel more hatred for him at the thought of this shame than in imagining him making love to Liz behind those shutters. As if my anger at him had less to do with being false than with not being sufficiently true.

She has just come out. She crosses diagonally, turns the corner, and heads toward the Champs-Elysées, taking the sunny side of the street. I emerge from my doorway recess, follow her at a distance in the crowd of tourists. She's wearing a sexy tailored suit that I've never seen before, her raincoat over her shoulders. She seems carefree, peers into shop windows, fixes her hair in the reflection, discreetly verifying if men are turning back to look at her. I've never seen her like this. She, so rigid, so inhibited outside of bed . . . She cuts over to Avenue de Marigny, quickens her step when she notices the time.

A man bumps into me, a high-strung body-building type. He stops and asks for an apology. I push him away and step over the papers he dropped. I start to walk faster, my eyes fixed on the silhouette cutting a channel under the chestnut trees, when he grabs my arm and demands in a louder voice that I apologize. The next moment I see him bent in two on the ground. I can't get over my strength, the precision of that karate chop that escaped me like a reflex. Apart from pull-ups when I climb trees, I never have time to exercise. The same way I never learned to play the piano.

I slip away as a small group forms around the hulk writhing on the sidewalk. I slalom between groups of people and cars, run across the street toward the Marigny theater. The line at the ticket window makes me step off the curb. Camera-trucks linked by cables hide the intersection. I widen my stride, stop short at the flow of cars rushing toward the Arc de Triomphe, search in every direction. I've lost her.

Suddenly I see her hair disappearing into the subway. I run after her, hurtle down the steps, find her just as she heads toward the La Défense platform. She takes the corridor where violinists are playing and suddenly breaks into a run. I think that she's spotted me, but maybe it's only because the departure signal has sounded. She jumps into the packed train. I rush in just as the doors close, catch my breath as I look over my fellow passengers. She is standing not twenty yards from me. I don't know if she's seen me, if she's trying to lose me, or if she's simply running late.

At every stop, I elbow through people to make

sure she hasn't gotten off. The third stop is the one. I see her walk quickly toward the Avenue de la Grande-Armée exit, cut over to the side marked 'Even numbers'. Not once has she stopped to check her path. Either she has already come this way, or she's leading me around.

She hurries to street level, buttons up her raincoat against the risen wind, heads down the avenue, and turns into a one-way street. She stops in front of a hotel and suddenly turns around. I sensed it one second earlier and hid behind a trunk. Her eyes sweep over the sidewalk, but don't come as far as my tree. She goes in.

I run up to the building facade, which I skirt closely, my forehead pressed against the windows, trying to make out the interior through the curtains. It's a bar. I see her hesitate at the entrance, then walk toward the tables near the counter. I immediately pull back, head toward the doorman spinning the revolving door. I cross the lobby like a guest of the hotel, go up to the bar entrance and pretend to study the menu. Liz is sitting at a corner table, next to a young guy of about twenty with an evil smile and a sleeveless leather jacket. A huge camera is resting on the small table next to his glass. He shows it to her proudly, puts his arm around her neck. Suffocating, I see her offer him her lips, give him a passionate kiss, a kiss of reunion. Just like the one she shares with the stranger in my dream about Sixth Avenue, beneath the figure of the national debt.

A maître d' comes toward me. I beat a retreat, go back to the linden tree that hid me before. The jealousy I'm feeling is not even violent. It's an abyss, a freefall. How many lovers does she have? How many men is she going to bring into my life? Is the one she moved into Rue de Duras already not enough for her? How many times is she going to kill me in someone else's arms? She's sick, she has certainly gone insane, and it smoldered during all those years of silence, spats, depression hidden beneath conjugal boredom. I know what the breaking point was – the slap over the *Jenny Jones Show* – but what is the real root of the problem? Getting fired from her law office, for which she never gave me a convincing reason? My expeditions without her to every forest on earth? Or the routine of my hours in the lab fifty miles from our home? Every time I found her acting strange, in the evening, she fended off my questions by asking me how my research was coming, and she looked so fascinated at first that I didn't even see the subterfuge. I told her about my insights, my experiments, my amazing discoveries; she seemed thrilled, and it was enough to reassure me about her. Convinced that I was her dream man, I slept peacefully.

The photographer leaves first, with a half-smile, his camera over his shoulder. He straddles a scooter marked 'Press'. Three minutes later, she leaves the hotel in turn and heads back toward the subway, with the same expression as when she arrived. I follow in her steps, automatically, without trying to understand where this boy came from, why their meeting was so short, why she seems so indifferent, concerned only with her image in the shop windows.

I speed up to overtake her, then change my mind. Not here. Not as someone trailing her. Not in a position of strength.

At Champs-Elysées-Clémenceau, I get off the instant the doors open, run as fast as I can to the exit, and stop at the end of the platform in front of a vending machine, which I lean against. I hunch over, arms folded, giving myself the extinguished look of someone who has been there for hours, who isn't waiting for anything in particular, who has lost all hope. I spot her raincoat in the crowd. I raise my eyes as she approaches, notice her as if in surprise.

'Liz!'

She freezes. She didn't jump, or barely. She lets a group of people pass, then comes up to me. I can see in her eyes that she's going to call me 'sir', ask me to leave her alone or she'll yell for the cops.

'I've understood, Liz. I know why you're doing this.'

Her face relaxes. Then she frowns, suppresses a gesture of annoyance, pretends not to follow. Four completely contradictory ways of reacting. As if it were up to me to choose, validate one of these possible attitudes.

'Why I'm doing what?'

The question doesn't commit her to anything, asked in a neutral tone that can mean resentment just as well as defiance. I plunge forward, in one burst.

'You don't know me anymore, you've replaced me, fine. We had become strangers, it's true.

The only thing still holding us together was our memories, everything that was strong between us in the beginning. So suddenly you have a chance to destroy all that and you go for it: you erase me, deny me, okay, but why, Liz? Why? To give me back my freedom, or to make me realize what I'm losing?'

There is no support in the look she gives me, no echo. She listens, registers, waits.

'I'm asking your forgiveness, Elizabeth. I can change. I'm going to prove to you that I can be different. Just give me a chance . . .'

'Did you come from the apartment?'

That's all she's worried about. I've got it now. I shake my head, tell her that I didn't dare try to force my way in again, go through more hostility, rejection, ridicule. She digs her hands into the pockets of her raincoat, looks for the truth in my eyes. She wants to make sure I haven't seen the impostor again. Or that I didn't follow her. My disarmed look, making no claim and ready to do anything to get back in her good graces, should comfort her.

'What's all this bullshit?'

She has spoken in a low voice, her head to one

side, almost as if she were addressing another part
of me. She insists:

'What game are you playing? Are you fucking
with me? You getting even?'

Her tone is clear, without hostility, without reproach, with an incomprehension that sounds
authentic. Once more I lose my footing.

'Liz . . . am I your husband or not?'

She makes no sign of impatience, no movement
to leave, none of the reactions I would have expected. She stares at me, undecided, serious. As if
she had to think before answering the question,
deciding what her behavior should be. She suddenly grabs me by the wrist, with a vigor that takes
me back years.

'I can't, Martin.'

'You can't *what*?'

She looks around, nervous.

'I don't have a choice.'

'Is he threatening you? Is that it?'

She nods, her lips shut.

'If you don't play along, he'll come after you?
Is he making you talk? But what about?'

'I can't answer that.'

'And who is he?'

'I can't tell you anything, Martin. It's bigger than us. All I want is for us both to get out in one piece. All right?'

The mix of supplication and hope in her voice leaves me shattered. She's saying whatever comes into her head, she's improvising; I don't get the feeling she's in danger. On the other hand, she seems genuinely concerned for me. It even appears she's trying to protect me.

'What am I supposed to do, Liz?'

'Lie low, just until Saturday, and everything will be okay.'

'Why Saturday?'

'I'll explain everything afterward, but keep out of sight until then, don't talk to anyone, don't try to prove who you are. Promise?'

'So what's the goal? To keep me from working at the INRA against GMOs?'

A shudder that she suppresses, a hesitation in her eye, once again. Like incredulity.

I venture, 'I mean, this is crazy! There are easier ways of keeping me quiet. No? Unless it's something else. If it's not Monsanto, then who is it?'

She gives my arm a squeeze, then lets her hand drop.

'We'll get out of this, Martin, I promise. But stay out of sight. I love you.'

And she is perfectly believable. Her eyes crinkling, lips pressed together, chin quivering. I remember her kissing the photographer, letting him rub up against her. I say, 'All right.'

'Do you need money?'

She has already opened her handbag, slips her credit card into my pocket.

'Where did you sleep?'

I give a vague wave toward the benches on which bums continue to sleep off their night. She sighs, shaking her head, as if she blamed me for the situation I've gotten into because of her.

'Get a room at the Terrass.'

Those two syllables bring back the hotel on the corner above the Montmartre cemetery, the suite where we made love for twenty-four hours straight. It was our first trip to Paris. Our first vacation as lovers. I see her again in panties and a shirt, yesterday morning, standing in the hall, looking at me like some mistake. I see the other man in my pajamas, telling me to leave her alone and throwing me out of their home . . .

'I want to know one thing, Liz. Is it because of me, or because of him?'

'Of him?'

'Is he someone you were seeing, who wormed his way into your life by blackmail? Did you discover when it was too late that he was unbalanced, some guy who thought he was me, who wanted to get rid of me so he could take my place?'

She turns away, tightens her lips while staring at the train arriving at the platform across the tracks. I sense that I've hit the mark – or else she's trying to make me believe I did, to divert me from Monsanto. She hasn't answered any of my questions. And she gave me her Visa card so they can trace me if I use it.

'Let me handle this. I'll meet you Saturday at the Terrass. Trust me, Martin.'

A final glance, deep into my eyes, as if to reawaken everything that once bound us together. That expression, that glimmer of appeal . . . I don't understand. It's not love, but friendship. The memory of complicity, of unspoken understanding, of fraternity through thick and thin. The opposite of our story. Of our passion that died from misunderstanding, deceit, pretense.

I suddenly clasp her to me, crush my lips against her mouth. She kisses me casually, studiously, with good will. Nothing. I don't recognize anything, not her tongue, not her body pressed against mine, nor the hands frozen on the nape of my neck. I have a clone in my arms. A clone with no emotion, no desire, no reference points. A robot who kisses me as if I were the photographer from a while ago, or the stranger under the national debt . . . It's exasperating. I feel like smacking her, like that Monday morning in Greenwich, the only time I ever raised a hand to her.

'What are you thinking about?'

I tell her. She raises her eyebrows. I give her my version of the fight, damning myself as much as I can, in the hope of lessening the violence I feel toward her. She listens to me, eyes staring, lips parted. It's as if she doesn't remember the scene. In spite of myself, I brush aside her fringe. The scar is where it should be.

'Get a grip on yourself, goddammit!' she hisses, shaking me. 'This isn't the time!'

'Then where did you get that scar?'

Her eyes narrow.

'A sliver of glass, in Manhattan, on October second. Okay? The eyeglasses. You with me?'

'It was the lamp in the living room, Liz. When I pushed you down. Why do you refuse to . . . ?'

'Enough!'

The people waiting on the platform look at us with curiosity, distrust, fatigue.

'Go to the Terrass Hotel, Martin, I'm begging you. And wait for me there. I love you.'

She hasn't said that to me in eight years, and here this makes twice in five minutes. I watch her silhouette walk away under the vaulted ceiling, head to the exit stairs, return to its life without me. I was expecting anything, but not this reversal of the situation. She accused me in public of not being me, when she's the one who has become someone else. Aside from her looks and her perfume, she is nothing like the woman with whom I spent the last decade.

I dig for a coin, slide it into the vending machine, swallow a Coke in small gulps with my eyes closed. What is she trying to do? Neutralize me, mix me up, make me feel tender? She didn't follow up on anything, pursue any arguments or explain any of her statements; she gave only hints, and didn't even try to convince me. She merely echoed back my theories, telling me to lie low. The only time she seemed completely sincere was in that look of fraternal comradeship that isn't based on anything.

9

The secretary asked me to wait for a few moments. I've been sitting for a quarter of an hour between an iron sculpture and the court's ruling against a brand of cigarettes, framed under glass, with the amount of damages underlined in yellow.

The detective emerges from his office accompanying a female client, comes back to apologize to the man who showed up after me: he'll be with him in three minutes. He points me to his office.

I leave the waiting room with a bad feeling that is verified as soon as the bald man sits down. He pulls a file from the stack at his left, opens it, and states in a neutral tone, 'You don't exist.'

I look straight back at him, my mouth dry. He spreads out the documents before him and continues.

'What should I begin with? Your birth? No one named Martin Harris came into the world on 9 September 1960.'

I reply, sitting in the chair that he hasn't offered me, 'And who told you that?'

'Public records. Nor did any Franklin and Susan Harris work at Disney World or at Coney Island. You did not marry Elizabeth Lacarrière on 13 April 1992, in Greenwich. Number 255 Sawmill Lane, where you claim to live, is in fact a sawmill, and the Environmental Science Center on Sachem Street at Yale, whose laboratory you've supposedly headed since 1990, was not even built until last year. Shall I go on?'

Huddled against the armrest, a cold sweat in my collar, I open my mouth to defend myself. He takes another document.

'The legal department of Monsanto has never heard of you. On the other hand, we found five treatises on botany published under the name of Martin Harris, as well as his deposition concerning testimony from plants, given before the court of Madison, Wisconsin, in 1998 – except that Martin Harris died the following year. Your social security number corresponds to a man with the same name, an electrician in Kansas.'

He raises his eyes, rests his elbows on the papers, and joins his fingertips.

'In short, you were never born, your family doesn't exist, none of your colleagues recognized your photo, and your botanical discoveries were made by someone else.'

He closes my file and pushes it toward me.

'Conclusion: you owe me one thousand three hundred euros. I'd prefer it in cash.'

I stand up, regain my wits, and tell him there must be some mistake.

'That's not my problem. You hired me to verify information, my correspondents have done so, I'm handing you the proof, and here is my invoice: you pay it and we're done. The rest is none of my concern, is that clear? The report is yours to do with as you please. I have no wish to know what kind of scam you're trying to pull, or if you're just some joker who likes to waste people's time. Pay up and get out.'

Calmly, my hands raised, my tone reasonable, I try to explain to him that the results of his investigation confirm the thesis of a plot against me: they have erased my existence even in the government's computers . . . But nothing moves on his face. I undo the strap of my Rolex and place it on his desk.

'If this is as fake as the rest . . .'

I don't answer. He picks up the watch, turns it over, looks for the hallmark, puts it in his drawer. It was worth four thousand dollars six months ago, for my tenth wedding anniversary.

'Goodbye, Mr Harris. And congratulations on your acting talent. You missed your calling.'

I stand up, take the documents, and leave as he starts into the next file. My hand on the doorknob, I turn around.

'Are you sure about your investigators?'

'What would we get out of lying to you?'

I walked in the streets, mechanically, without seeing anything, my head empty, squeezing under my arm the file that reduced my forty years on this earth to nothing. The rain fell harder and harder. I went into a McDonald's, bought some fries, and took some paper napkins to wipe off the file. I read the research reports, the investigators' notes. Everything was false. Leaving aside the mistakes in my personal information, intentional or not, nothing corresponded to my memory, and I knew *that* was correct. A recollection can be mistaken, one can interpret reality, lie to oneself, but not when it concerns the basic touchstones of one's life or the details that support them.

One aberration among so many others: the investigator claims that, of the two Figure 8s at Coney Island, the Thunderbolt was the one they demolished, and the Cyclone has been classified an historic monument since 1991. I don't know how he could have confused the two, but for me it's as if he had said that the Twin Towers were still standing, and that the terrorists had destroyed the Empire State Building. I can still see the surroundings, the decrepit charm of Coney Island at dawn with its closed rides, the seagulls flying around the yellow-and-red pylon of the Parachute Jump, the teenagers between fixes, and the old Russians in electric wheelchairs rolling toward the dock with their fishing rods. I see the roped-up workmen unbolting the Cyclone's rails, my father's desolate look in the square of plastic turf in front of the brick house as he watched the last scrap of his life being dismantled. Watchman over a closed ride. Responsible for a heap of scrap iron sold by the ton that the steel mills would come fetch someday.

At first I think the investigator simply hasn't bothered visiting the sites, but next in the list of errors he claims to have discovered comes John Dewey High School. He's turned the wooden school building on the edge of the dunes into a brown warehouse surrounded by barbed wire, between the elevated train and the air-conditioned tenements of South Brooklyn. Why this confusion? Carelessness, or a deliberate attempt to blur my reference points, my awareness of the past, my internal logic? What he's describing is Rubinstein and Klein, the department store opposite Bay 50th Street station on the W line, where I worked for two months before my father got me the job at Nathan's. I know better than he does – it's my life! I'm the one who spent all those years between Coney Island and the depths of Brooklyn: those graffitied walls next to a river of garbage, those trailers next to the houses beneath dented air conditioners, those fire escapes that crumble into rust when you're kissing beneath them – that's *my* youth! Who does this nameless person think he is to challenge my past and mix up all the names, dates, and places? And if he did it on purpose, then why?

As for my department at Yale that supposedly wasn't built until 2001, I give up. Could I have dreamed all those mornings for eleven years when I parked my Ford next to the Old Campus and walked up the hill to the Environmental Science Center, beneath the maple trees of Hillhouse Avenue? Could I have lived all those years in a sawmill without realizing it, married to a woman I never wed?

There's at least one positive side to these three pages of denials: if my biography is only a heap of lies and deceptions, then the man living in Paris with my name is as much a fake as I am. It gives me a brief feeling of revenge against those who chose to believe *him*, but it doesn't change the problem. The proof that *that* Martin Harris is false doesn't make me any more authentic. For some reason I can't fathom, this report makes us both out to be impostors. But I don't believe so much confusion can be unintentional. How can I explain that no one recognized my picture, in Greenwich or at Yale, other than by the investigator's ill will? The question is to know who is trying to erase my existence, remove my life from the record, destroy me in the eyes of the world — and destroy me *in duplicate*.

I raise my eyes. All around me, young people

are devouring Big Macs dripping lettuce and pickles, giving only a vague glance at the guy absorbed in his papers as his fries grow cold. I need to clear my head of all the memories crowding in in response, which are scattering my thoughts, mixing up ages and places . . . I have to put them back in order, so that I can answer point for point. I return to the first page and, pen squeezed between my thumb and the bandage, I begin writing down the course of my life, my truth about the minor details and key events.

Half an hour later, I've filled the backs of the report's three pages. And, while I'm still sure of myself as to the content, I've begun to have doubts about the form. The disproportion is glaring. I am extremely precise about unimportant points, and suddenly there are three years that I don't know how to fill. And that's not all. To show that he's earned his fee, the detective has noted as an addendum the date corresponding to the national debt that I see in my dream. It's October second of last year. The date Liz mentioned this morning when I brought up her scar. And I can't find a single thing that I did on October second. It's a complete blank.

Perhaps it's still the effects of the coma, the excess of glutamate that has hypertrophied certain memories at the expense of others. Or just a lack of attention, moral wear, the routine in which everyone ends up shutting himself, even those who think they're sheltered behind a passion. My passion for plants has protected only my capacity for work; emotionally, my life is a disaster under an orderly facade, a banal failure, a sum total of misery that I'd be better off forgetting.

I push away the papers, heartsick. I no longer have the strength or the will to go surf the internet to support my arguments, prove my good faith, denounce the lies . . . Why not simply let go, draw a line through this waste, start my life over somewhere else – or throw myself without remorse into the Seine, where I should have stayed? Everyone is lying to me, no one needs me, I'm a nuisance to everyone, and I no longer have the heart to fight.

In the midst of these customers who walk around with their trays, waiting for me to give up my spot, one face takes shape, one voice holds me back. The only person who believed in me, who held out her hand to me without second thoughts, who was kind to me for nothing. I go downstairs to the toilets, pick up the wall phone under the cries of a baby being changed. Muriel answers on the second ring.

'Martin, at last! I've been waiting two hours for you to call! I've got some great news!'

I'm about to share her joy, but she continues:

'I got hold of your assistant, he finally answered . . .'

'Rodney Cole?'

'And to top it off, he speaks French. I couldn't believe it! He was floored to hear what's happened to you. He's like you, he can't understand what your wife is up to, but it seems she's been in a state of depression for months. He's a really nice guy. He said, "I'm putting together all the proof that Martin is who he says he is and I'm taking the next plane." He'll be here in the morning.'

'Wait, wait a minute, Muriel . . . You described what I look like?'

'Of course! And the other shithead as well. Listen, you're not going to start having second thoughts just when we're finally getting proof, are you?'

Her 'we' echoes in the noise of traffic on the

other end of the line. I shut my eyes to block the tears.

'I get off at four. I'll pick up Sébastien at school and we'll meet up at my house, okay? You still have the address?'

'Yes. And what about Rodney?'

'Tomorrow morning, nine o'clock, at the Sofitel near Porte Maillot. Is that all right?'

I murmur my thanks, hang up, and lean my head against the wall. I've spent so many hours vainly struggling against this absurdity that, now that reality is finally siding with me, I have a hard time believing it. Why should that upstart Rodney, with his prudent vigilance, his calculated slowness, suddenly go through so much trouble for me, when he didn't even recognize my picture? That said, I don't recall his name being mentioned, other than in my list of people to contact.

I run back upstairs, feverishly search through the papers I left on the table. At no point does the investigator specify just who at Yale was shown my photo. No names, just 'his colleagues in the botany department', 'the dean of his department' – every time, the moron went to the School of Forestry and Environmental Studies on Prospect

Street, which is vying with us for research credits. They obviously mistook him for a reporter, and no one at Forestry was about to talk me up. They even fed him the line that the Environmental Science Center was only a year old, to deter him from going there to pursue his research. The dean must have wowed him with his prestigious seniority, the dusty credit of his archives, the success levels of his privileged students, his corny lecture program, and the idiot was completely dazzled.

I fold the sheets with a vengeful smile, imagining Muriel's reactions to this report, this monument to deception and ineptitude that ultimately pays me homage by trying to wipe me out. I'm eager to see her, to find myself in her eyes as she sees me. Too bad she isn't a bit sexier; the desire left in me by the shop girl at Tendance D rises in my throat, with all these high-school girls with their Big Macs chattering around me. So many years of frustration, scruples, repressed desire under the elms of the Old Campus, when the curvy silhouettes of the co-eds and their well-bred smiles stood out against the Gothic facades . . . All those temptations overcome to remain true to my image as a respectable professor. Whatever the outcome of my present situation, I no longer want any part of that life.

10

'You know when I knew for sure you were the real one? When you told us about the hydrangeas identifying the killer. And then when the other guy talked about his childhood. He was just reciting his memories, but you were re-living them in your eyes: your father trimming shrubs into Mickey Mouse, the hot-dogs, the Figure 8 . . . I'm so happy, Martin! You want some jam?'

It's beautiful to see a woman being reborn. She has been transformed by my story, by the role she's played in it, by the trust she was right to place in me against all odds. I don't object. The investigator's report has stayed in my pocket. I see her become almost pretty, because for the first time in her life she hasn't been jerked around, and the wrinkles around her lips have disappeared under her smile, her enthusiasm, and the hunks of baguette she's sharing with me.

Her son watches us, perplexed. We have invited ourselves into his after-school snack, on the kitchen table. I've discovered a ravenous hunger in myself and we've already gobbled down an entire loaf of bread, alternating butter, marmalade, pâté, and Nutella. All the doubts and anxieties I've introduced into this manless apartment on the third floor of a miserable high-rise – what do they matter? This evening, I've decided to be the man that Muriel imagines.

'Tell Seb about your job.'

I like the informality of her tone, which comes spontaneously now that she's sure about me. I tell Sébastien how I grew tomatoes in the desert without a drop of water, just by playing music for them. I had transposed into sound frequencies the quantum signal emitted by their proteins, and I blasted them with it from amplifiers, in the form of a vegetal rap that acted like a growth hormone. His eyes widen above his bowl as his hot chocolate grows cold. He's a boy caught between childhood and acne, with a black fuzz connecting his eyebrows and his kid's voice still intact.

'I've been recording him,' Muriel confides with a sad smile, as soon as he's left the kitchen to go play on his computer. 'I tape his voice all the time, without telling him. I want to hold onto it.

His friends' voices are already breaking – it's horrible.'

'He seems like a sweet kid.'

'He's incredibly gifted, but lousy in school. He finds it boring. But he always comes in first in the IQ tests. And because of that, he gets beaten up by everybody and falls even more behind. I don't know how he's going to turn out. I don't have enough money to put him in a private school.'

I nod gravely. I like this life around me, this concrete life, thick, enclosed, this mix of insignificant little dramas and daily wear and tear, without horizons or false promises. A life of trimesters and months' ends, encircled solitude, miles driven in isolation and time spent waiting at airports, passengers taken on and empty return trips. A life of hours stolen from work to devote them to the kids, a sacrifice without issue, a cause lost in advance.

Her daughter arrives. Seventeen, tall and pretty, detached, with a distant air but a frank gaze. Indifferent and polite. Her name is Morgane, and she smells of ammonia, permanents, and synthetic lilac. An apprentice hairdresser. She downs an apple juice with her back against the fridge, lets us finish our snack with a 'ciao', and heads into her room to listen to techno.

Muriel watches me eat, cheek in her hand.

'So, this is my life,' she comments soberly. 'I adore them, but you did a rotten thing to me. Since yesterday, I can't stop thinking about how I'd react if I came home one evening to find another woman in my place.'

'There's always a way to prove who you are, Muriel.'

'Yeah, right – I'd wish her good luck and be out that door like a bat out of hell!'

She snorts with laughter while biting her lips, waves her hand to annul the blasphemy, and finishes her tea with a grimace.

'I never have time in my life to just sit still. And so much the better, I guess. A little glass of Cinzano?'

Without transition, we push away our cups and move on to the aperitif. She tells me about her childhood, her marriage, her divorce. None of it is interesting, all of it can be predicted from the start, but the rage to try to climb out of it all alone, to spare her children what she has lived through, the energy spent for nothing, give this

whole banal wasteland the dimensions of a Greek
tragedy.

The clock hits the hour and her kid comes back
in to ask when dinner is. She tells him to fend for
himself; this is her night off. I offer to take them
to a restaurant and they look at me as if I were
from Mars. Morgane, telephone glued to her ear,
comes in to announce she's spending the night at
Virginie's. Her mother holds out her hand; she
hands over the phone with a sigh, turning on her
heels. Muriel verifies the alibi, hangs up, shrugs
her shoulders, saying that in any case she's been
on the pill for six months, and what's the use of
going to bed early to be well rested for a job you
can't stand?

'Pick out something from the freezer,' she says
to her son as she finishes off her third Cinzano.

I ask her what Rodney's voice sounded like on
the phone.

'Normal. He has a lot of respect for you, in any
case. He must have asked me twenty times how
you were taking it, if you were holding up, what
you were planning to do about your wife . . .'

'You talked to him on his cell?'

'I redialed the number in the call log. So what

are you going to do about your wife? And the people who are doing this to you?'

'I don't know.'

'Anyway . . .'

She leaves her sentence unfinished above her glass. The beginnings of drunkenness lessen the euphoria, pull her away from my story, push her further into a reality that she will never escape once my problem is solved. Tomorrow I'll have proof of my existence, I'll head off to do what I have to do, and for her there will be nothing new anymore . . . I can follow all these thoughts on her face, between the uneven locks sticking out of her hair clips. I've been a blast of wind through her life, a rush of madness, a burst of folly, and now everything is about to settle back into place, only worse.

She stretches a hand out to the bottle, knocking over her glass. I jump up too late. She says she's sorry, tells me where the bathroom is, plunges her head into her crossed arms.

I exit the room out of tact. Morgane is putting on makeup in front of the drugstore mirror; she says to come in, I won't bother her. I go to turn on the faucet, dab at the stains on my jacket.

She looks at the bandages peeling off my right hand.

'Does that hurt?'

'It's nothing, it's healing all by itself.'

She draws a line with her eyeliner pencil, advises me to use a poultice made of bread dough and sea salt.

'My dad's with a woman who has horses. When I went to their place, I used to fall all the time. Sea salt is the bomb for edemas.'

I thank her.

'You known Mom a long time?'

Perhaps Muriel didn't tell them about our accident. I answer, 'Yes.' And it's true that part of me could have known her at twenty, led a similar existence, started this kind of family . . . Our points of departure are very similar.

'You seem to be good for her.'

She attacks the other eye, asks if we're just friends. I nod while rubbing the fabric with soap. A telephone rings in the other room.

'She's really great, you know? My dad did a number on her. Since then we're all she's got. I'm sick of seeing her by herself.'

I concentrate on the spots on my jacket. She

puts down her eyeliner pencil, comes closer to get a tube from the sink.

'Don't you like her?'

I return her gaze as she looks hard at my silence. There is a real reproach in her eyes, a genuine admiration for the mother she must have hated before coming to understand her.

'Sure I like her, but . . .'

Her lips purse at my ellipsis. Then, with a sigh, she removes her T-shirt and unbuttons her jeans. With her breasts bared, she goes to choose a dress from the closet, which she puts on facing away from me.

'Well, see you,' she says, turning back at the door with a smile.

I remain frozen in the middle of the tile floor, dumbfounded by that gesture, her tactful abruptness, the way she used her body to arouse my desire for her mother.

'Martin!'

Muriel calls to me against the sound of the apartment door slamming. I join her in the living room. She's standing against the bookshelves, her phone at her ear.

'Thanks, I'll tell him. Love to Ginette, and get

some rest. That was Robert,' she says, hanging up. 'The friend who lent me his taxi. He just got back from vacation and he called the cops. They found the truck that ran us into the river. At the bottom of a garbage dump in the Eure-et-Loir. And guess what? It was stolen!'

She's thrilled. She hopes the fact that she refused right of way to a stolen truck will help with the insurance and license revocation. I don't respond. I stand there, pondering the old, damaged books lined up on the shelves. Something stirs in my memory, which I try to isolate – a regret, a loss, an association of ideas ... I don't know if the connection is with Muriel's words or with the smell of basement and damp leather permeating the room.

'Inherited from my parents,' she says, following my gaze. 'The entire history of world religions since people first invented God as an excuse to beat the crap out of each other. They're dust collectors and full of germs, but I can't bring myself to chuck them out. My folks were so proud of them. Memory really sucks.' She uncorks a bottle of white, then continues, 'When you came to, I thought you'd be a total amnesiac. I said to myself, what luck.'

Sébastien brings us square fish with soggy breadcrumbs and some kind of tomato roughage, which we eat at the coffee table while watching the news. Floods, peace plans, assassinations, soccer, an oil slick, the official visit of the American president, the British queen's woes. Muriel fumes about the traffic jams, lists the month's nuisances: three heads of state, twelve demonstrations, the closing of the riverside lanes . . . You can't even get around Paris anymore. And to top it off, the mayor is cementing the bus lanes; now the taxis can't even pull out when a delivery truck is in the way. I listen distractedly, grunt agreement as I eat.

'What are you thinking about, Martin? You look like something's bothering you.'

'Not really, I was just wondering why we took the Seine road to go to the airport. I'm starting to learn my way around Paris, and . . . well, it's not the most direct route.'

She stares at me, looking tense. I pretend to forget about it by concentrating on the weather forecast. I wouldn't want her to think I was accusing her of taking a roundabout way just to pad the fare.

'What do you mean, "not the most direct"?'

'Nothing. It's just that taking the Seine to go to Charles-de-Gaulle from my place . . .'

'From your place? You mean Rue de Duras? That's not where I picked you up!'

'Then where *did* you pick me up?'

She snatches up the remote, mutes the sound. 'In Courbevoie.'

'Where?'

'Courbevoie,' she repeats, as if it were self-evident. 'Boulevard Saint-Denis.'

I feel like the wind has been knocked out of me.

'But . . . what was I doing all the way out there?'

Her gesture indicates that I'm the one who should know. I rack my brain, but come up blank.

'Are you sure?'

She confirms it, mollified, and asks if this is the first memory that hasn't come back to me. I remain vague.

'We're watching M6,' her son decides, picking up the remote.

He surfs through the channels, turns the volume back up. Muriel reminds him that he has school at eight o'clock. He settles between us on the yellow couch, and we watch a group of girls who are getting coached on how to sing and dishing dirt on each other for the camera, each one trying to have the others eliminated by the TV audience so she'll become the newest pop idol. The kid gobbles up this phantasmagoria, vibrating with enthusiasm for an androgynous-looking black girl and calling the others skanks. When his sobbing candidate is wiped out in the next phone poll, he flings down the remote and leaves the room. I stay behind with Muriel, an empty cushion between us. I've spent the program replaying the entire scene in my head: we arrived at Rue de Duras, I was treated at the pharmacy, I joined Liz at France Télécom, we went to sit in the café with our suitcases, I discovered I'd forgotten my laptop, I ran after Muriel's taxi, yelling for it to stop . . . It's true that I can't visualize the surroundings at that point, but how could I possibly have ended up in Courbevoie?

'Would it be too much if I asked you to read him a story?'

I look at her in surprise.

'I know he's a bit old for it, but since his father, no one's ever . . . Never mind,' she decides, changing the channel. 'It's too late anyway.'

I get up, rest a hand on her shoulder to keep her from stopping me. Sébastien is lying on his stomach, calves sticking up, absorbed in a comic book. Monsters and soccer stars paper the walls. He says I can sit and check out the books if I want; he doesn't mind. I walk up to a small aquarium sitting on a shelf, with two ratty fish and three pathetic pebbles in a decor of algae.

'Hey, you've got achlaia.'

He raises an eye, asks what *that* is.

'A bisexual algae. When it reproduces, it gives the fish magnificent colors.'

'Then this one's junk. See how brown they are?'

'That's because the filaments aren't touching. In achlaia, puberty is triggered by contact with the other sex. Yours are going to remain children their entire life if you leave them like that.'

I plunge my fingers into the dirty water, push together the pebbles to glue the pale-green blades together between them. He has left his bed, listens to me with a curious face while staring at the bowl.

'Until they're in each other's presence, they'll have no identity. But after that, they can change to suit whoever they meet, become male or female depending on the attraction . . .'

'So you're saying my algae are homos?'

'Transsexual. The advantage they have over humans is that they can change sex as often as they like. It depends on who they're in love with.'

'I thought they were dead.'

'They were just waiting for you to pay attention to them.'

At the doorway, Muriel watches us leaning over the aquarium. There are tears in her eyes. Sébastien turns around and she disappears. He gets back into bed, asks me how I decided to go into my field.

'The blue leaves.'

'The what?'

I'm just as startled as he is. I don't know why I said that, or what those words mean. There are no blue leaves in nature. Except in certain conifers, but those are called needles.

'Did you already know when you were my age?' he pursues.

'Yes. I think so.'

'Wow, you're lucky. I don't know what I want to do. Everything's blocked off, anyway.'

I give him a small smile of understanding, solidarity; I approach the bed, then hesitate. I don't know if you still kiss a boy that age goodnight. He holds out his hand, I shake it, and leave the room repeating the two words in my head. *Blue leaves* . . . The liquid sound calls up hazy images, scraps of voices that blend together, fall short.

I join Muriel in the living room. She is sitting on the floor in front of the dark television.

'He seemed to like that. I don't know what you were telling him . . .'

'Whatever came into my head; the result is what counts. The algae in his aquarium are just ordinary mold, but from now on he'll look at them like potential couples, teenagers trying to find themselves.'

My frankness shocks her, or my tact.

'Are you making a special effort for me, or are you always like this?'

I answer with an indecisive sigh.

'You never had any kids?'

'No.'

She stands up, saying that's a shame for them. She looks at the time.

'Do you have a place to sleep?'

'No.'

'Want the couch?'

'Thanks.'

She goes into her room, comes back with a pillow and a blanket. I haven't moved.

'Is everything all right, Martin?'

'I'm not sure. I'm wondering about a lot of things.'

'Me too.'

We look at each other, disarmed. She sets down the pillow, spreads out the blanket. She comes toward me. I take her in my arms, and we try to forget the rest.

Liz kisses him, gently pushes him back. Under the parading numbers in lights, she gives a little wave of goodbye, the promise of a next time. She moves away. He straightens his glasses, goes to climb into his limousine parked next to the curb. His head explodes and he falls backward.

I wake up with a start, blink, look around me. I'm in a mauve room; a ray of light is coming through the window shades. Voices echo in the next room.

I pull up the quilt, which smells of lovemaking and fabric softener. I roll over on my stomach, dampen the noise in the crook of my elbow, my ear pressed into the pillow. The night was violent and tender, so strong and at the same time so simple . . . We were like two kids stifling their cries of pleasure because of the parents. It wasn't like anything I've ever known, and yet I don't feel any different; something comes back together inside me, falls back into place after years of contortions. I liked sex with Liz because it made her into another woman; she overcame her coldness, her anger, listened only to her body. She forgot herself when making love. Muriel, in giving herself, finds herself again. I discovered her to be carefree, playful, and tender, as she would be all the time if life gave her a little breathing room. She's a damaged woman who repairs herself by loving, not a spoiled child who breaks her toys and wastes away. One week away from my daily routine and I no longer recognize myself: I feel completely removed from my choices, my concessions, my pretexts. I have been married to someone who is totally incompatible, counting on the nights when our bodies spoke to bridge the distance between us the rest of the time; to me, this seemed the true path of love. But it's easier to show love directly to someone who's close to you.

That said, I don't know who I'm going to find this morning, what Muriel is awaiting me across that wall. Maybe mornings after make her as melancholic as the return to normal life after two days of absurdity. I don't know if we'll pretend, if we'll simply not mention it, if we'll say we made a mistake, or if we'll want more. The morning following lovemaking is also a first time.

I put on my clothes and join Muriel in the kitchen. She is sitting at the table with an older man in a green windbreaker, who turns toward me and smiles warmly.

'I'm Robert,' he says. 'Glad to know you. And sorry to wake you up. I needed the taxi for a regular. Twice a year I drive her to her cure in Le Touquet. It's getting on seventeen years now.'

'Sébastien, it's twenty-five of!' Muriel calls out.

She finishes filling out an application form, signs it, and hands it to her colleague. She tells me that she, too, though she's not happy about it, is going to work for G7 Taxi – assuming they'll let her keep her license and put her on the waiting list.

'It's nuts to stay independent,' Robert insists, taking me as witness.

I nod, sit down. I see that life has taken over this morning, that the tender and unbridled woman from last night has gotten back into line. She serves me some coffee, asks if I slept well. I answer in a neutral tone.

'I can get you a car tomorrow. Antonio's going on sick leave 'cause he's got the flu.'

'His car's a piece of crap.'

'That's the stuff!' Robert grins, washing his hands in the sink. 'Okay, I'm off.'

They kiss on the cheek. Sébastien sticks his head in, knapsack on his shoulder, and asks if I'll be here tonight.

'Fifteen 'til!' his mother answers.

'Need a ride to school, Seb?'

'No, it's cool, the guys are waiting for me. See ya.'

He slams the front door. Muriel's phone rings; she answers, listens, asks Robert, who's zipping up his jacket, 'Eight-fifteen, Batignolles for Austerlitz. You on it?'

'No prob.'

She jots down the address, leaning on the edge of the table.

'I'm happy for her,' Robert murmurs, looking me in the eye, crushing my fingers.

He hasn't noticed the bandage and I swallow the pain with a friendly grimace. She gives him the address, hands him back the keys to his car. He sticks the folded application in his pocket and promises he'll pull any strings he can.

As soon as he leaves the apartment, Muriel jumps on me and holds me tight against her, breathes me in, kisses me, scratches my neck, holds me away to look at me.

'Was it all right for you?' she suddenly asks in a worried voice.

Without giving me time to answer, she drags me toward the bedroom, unbuttoning my shirt with a half-smile.

'Your meeting is in an hour, it'll take you ten minutes on the RER to Porte Maillot. That gives us forty-five minutes, if we're reasonable.'

She pushes me onto the bed, strips off her sweats, lies on top of me.

'You're not the same man when you make love,' she whispers in my ear.

She runs her tongue down my chest, slowly unbuckles my belt. Sound of an explosion.

She rushes to the window, rips aside the shade.

'Robert!' she screams.

Across the street, a car is engulfed in flames.

He is sitting behind a newspaper. The moment he sees me, he leaps from his armchair.

'It's all good, Martin. I have all the proof we need.'

Then he stops short, looks at me in alarm.

'What is it? What's wrong?'

I gaze steadily at him, trying to figure out his motive, to detect signs of a double-cross. Nothing: openness, energy, and the eagerness of a Boy Scout. Childlike eyes, receding hairline, hand on my shoulder.

'Now, tell me everything.'

I sit down. He retakes his seat, leaning forward, his forehead wrinkled by my troubles. I've waited for this moment for so long: to be vindicated by someone who knows me. And yet a certain unease prevents me from opening up to this man, who is almost the same age as I, whose surface respect and obsequiousness strike me as more artificial than ever. He's been scheming with the dean for years to take over my spot, and now this morning he arrives as my savior, with his character witness and pieces of evidence. I look for a suitcase next to him.

'I rented a car at the airport,' he says, anticipating my question. 'I stopped at a friend's place to shower and put the material somewhere safe.'

The bartender has come up to us, lets him finish his sentence before asking what we'd like. Rodney sends him away with an assertiveness I've never seen in him before.

'So really,' he says, 'Elizabeth is claiming you're not her husband? How do you explain that?'

'I talked to her, alone, yesterday morning. The guy pretending to be me is forcing her to lie, making her go along with it. Or maybe she's in on it, too, I have no idea . . .'

'Ms Caradet didn't say anything about that.'

'I didn't tell Ms Caradet everything. But she already knows too much – they've just blown up her car.'

He jumps, stares at me open-mouthed.

'They're out to kill us, Rodney.'

'When did this happen?'

'An hour ago.'

'Is she all right?'

I nod. She ran to get her son from school and her daughter at the salon; they're staying with a friend in a safe place. I made her promise not to use her cell phone.

'I can't believe Monsanto is *that* anxious to get you!' he protests.

Apparently Muriel gave him a complete report.

'Rodney . . . Does anyone else know you're in Paris?'

'A friend,' he says, lowering his eyes.

'Who?'

'The guy who's putting me up.'

'Can you vouch for him?'

Vague gesture, little pout. He's single. I've never heard about any relationship, but then I never took much of an interest in his private life.

'Did you tell him what's been happening to me?'

'No. I said I'd come to help out my boss, who was in some trouble, that's all.'

'I no longer exist, Rodney. They've made me disappear from the public record. They've erased my parents, my marriage. They're making it look as if Martin Harris from Yale died three years ago, and that my social security number belongs to an electrician in Kansas.'

'That's insane!'

'Unless it's the detective I hired . . . Maybe they paid him off to say that.'

'Let's go,' he says, standing up.

In front of the Sofitel, metal barriers prevent the cars from parking. Guards posted every twenty yards along Avenue des Ternes, red sash across their chests, await an official motorcade.

'The president is due to arrive at three,' Rodney whispers to me as we cross. 'You should have seen the security at the airport. The entire police force is out today.'

Between the lines: my personal problem hasn't exactly come at a convenient time. In Clichy, I saw the annoyed impatience of the cops inspecting the taxi's remains. Right now, a torched car in a rough neighborhood isn't their biggest concern. I let them keep their Molotov cocktail theory; I wasn't about to get myself hauled off to an interrogation room by suggesting it was a car bomb.

I walk three steps behind Rodney, up to a short street running perpendicular to the outer boulevard. I look behind me constantly, checking out the passers-by, verifying the doorways, the porches, the cars. He opens the door of a mini-van and I get in. I watch him pull out. We drive to the suburbs, beneath lampposts decorated with crossed flags. He throws me surreptitious glances while pretending to check the rearview. I don't believe he has any doubts about me, but he seems to be wondering if I have any about him.

'I admire you, Martin,' he states, crossing over a bridge.

'Why's that?'

'Your composure. Ms Caradet told me about your accident, the coma . . . And here you are, no different than before.'

'You think so?'

I'm perfectly aware that this is flattery, but his reflection touches me, all the more in that he's wrong. I no longer have anything in common with the repressed man who took refuge in plants to avoid life, who buried his human disappointments in vegetal passions. But I've suffered too much from the looks of others to stop pretending now.

'What exactly did you tell the police, Martin?'

'Who I was. But the other guy showed up

holding a passport with my name, and they threw out my complaint. We have to start from scratch, including the murder attempts. What proofs have you got that I'm me?'

'Profiles of you in the press, the tape of your interview on CBS, your parking pass at Yale, your diploma *honoris causa* from Bamako University, tax statements, telephone bills, expense reports, a photo of your parents . . . Whatever I could find in your desk.'

I frown.

'A photo of my parents?'

'Yes, and some of you with Liz.'

I nod, continue to verify in the vanity mirror that we're not being followed. I have no memory of keeping personal photos in my desk drawer. He must have searched through everything.

'We're almost there.'

He has left the crowded avenue and is now driving through a residential neighborhood, where construction sites alternate with old stone houses in various states of dilapidation. The surroundings seem vaguely familiar; an image floats toward the surface but can't quite get in focus. I don't know how to situate it, what to relate it to. It's as if my memory were working in a void. Or that it kept hitting an obstacle.

'How long have we known each other, Rodney?'

'A long time,' he smiles.

I'd like him to be more precise, but he seems to be trying to skirt the gaps in my memory out of tact, whereas I'm testing his own. Something about him doesn't ring true, but I don't know what. It's the same feeling as with Liz yesterday morning. And yet I know him so well. I wonder why I'm experiencing this defensive reflex, this strange distance . . .

'Did you go to the embassy?'

I answer that they tossed me out.

'And what about your colleague at the INRA? Haven't you been in touch with him again?'

'No – he believes the other guy.'

I've spied his reactions out of the corner of my eye. He looks relieved. But maybe he's just making a show of optimism to raise my spirits. The car enters a traffic circle, makes a left, drives another hundred yards down a sloping alley.

'Here we are,' he says, pressing a remote door-opener.

The mini-van passes through a gate covered

with yellowed wisteria. My gaze falls on the cracked stone pillar where the name of the villa is written: *The Blue Leaves*. A shock wave courses through my skull like a breaking dam as the car comes to a stop, an entire landscape forming. I close my eyes, press the back of my neck against the headrest, let the images fall into place.

'Is everything all right, Martin?'

'It's fine, I'm just tired. It'll pass.'

He falls silent. I open my eyes, recognize the graveled drive under the linden trees, the glassed-in steps he's parked in front of, the motorcycle chained to a willow.

'What an odd name, "blue leaves",' I say, with the casual smile of someone coming here for the first time. 'What does it mean?'

'I don't know. Maybe a writer used to live here, back when.'

The air is warm, the sounds muffled, the neighbors hidden by huge thujas that keep the neglected lawn in half-shadow. Our steps crackle on the dead leaves. Behind him, I climb the six steps to the terrace that I had hurtled down in the other direction. I rediscover how the door creaks as it scrapes on the floor tiles, the tint of the opaque windows against the black iron bars. And the smell, that mix of dampness and electric heating. The clanks of the expanding radiator above the ticking of the clock.

A young man in a tracksuit is making coffee in the kitchen. Rodney introduces us.

'This is Pascal, my Parisian friend. Professor Martin Harris.'

We greet each other, say we're delighted to meet. He's the fellow who asked me for a light the day before yesterday, in front of the police station.

'Would you like some coffee, professor?'

'I'd love some, thanks.'

'You like it strong?'

'Sure.'

The radio is broadcasting a tennis match. He fills a cup and hands it to me, explains that personally he likes it a lot weaker.

'And if you're hungry, please help yourself,' he continues with a cordial smile, showing me the breakfast already begun on the table.

'Excuse me for a moment,' says Rodney Cole.

He goes back out into the hall, opens a door under the staircase. I take a biscuit and spread butter on it, waiting for the sound of flushing.

When it starts, I walk toward Pascal, who is still pouring water into his filter and, exclaiming how good it is finally to feel like I'm in a climate I can trust, I slit his throat. Still talking, I muffle his cries, sit him in a chair against the wall, prop him up with the refrigerator door. The sports announcer salutes a magnificent volley, above the applause of the spectators. I wipe off the knife, slip it into the back of my trousers under my jacket, pick up my cup, and leave the kitchen just as Rodney comes out of the bathroom. I stop in the doorway. From where he is, he can't see the corner of the refrigerator. He looks tense; his smile is askew. He invites me to come upstairs and see the file he's assembled.

I climb the stairs behind him, cup in hand, remembering how I ran away from here eight days ago. Running across the lawn, through the streets of Courbevoie, Muriel's taxi crossing the avenue . . . All the details come together with clear precision.

Rodney Cole opens the door to a room filled with boxes, shows me a hirsute, corpulent man sitting at a table in a cloud of cigar smoke.

'Do you remember Dr Netzky?'

I say no, nod at the defector who worked on
me for three weeks at the conditioning center. A
leading light in the KGB, he put himself up for
auction in 1992. Beijing wanted him, Washington
got him.

'Incredible,' he murmurs, standing up.

He buttons his bulging jacket and comes closer.
The other man pulls out a Mauser and presses the
end of the silencer against my temple. I put on a
flabbergasted face.

'Rodney? What's got into you?'

He snickers. The several failures in his career
have always been linked to his ego, to under-
estimating his adversary.

'Sit down, Martin. I've got a surprise for you:
your name isn't Martin. And my name is Ralph
Channing. Does that ring a bell?'

I make it look like my knees are about to buckle,
so that he'll savor his little effect. He has always
picked names that retained his initials – the mark
of pride. He shoves me into a chair.

'Easy,' Netzky intervenes.

'Don't worry, I'm not going to break your little
creation,' retorts Ralph, straddling the seat facing
mine. 'Go on, then.'

With the barrel pointed vaguely at me, he watches the conditioner put down his cigar and come over to look deep into my eyes, murmuring in a slow voice, 'You will relax. When I count to four, you will be utterly relaxed. One: you're relaxing your mind, letting down your guard . . . At eight, you will return to the wakeful state that you are now leaving . . .'

I ask him what all this crap is about.

'Two: you are completely yourself, and everything is fine . . . Your consciousness is receding and following my voice. Three.'

He continues counting and I stop protesting. My eyes fixed and my mouth slack, I act like the model subject, the kind he's used to.

'You are now totally relaxed, you feel no more tension and, when you hear the number seven, I will tell you who you are and you will tell me if it's the truth. Seven. You are Martin Harris, botanist, husband of Elizabeth Lacarrière.'

'Yes.'

I've spoken without looking away, staring at his eyebrows.

'Incredible,' Netzky repeats.

'Is he faking it?'

'Why would he? If he ran out of here because he thought we were going to kill him, why would he walk back into the lion's den?'

'So then what *happened*?' Ralph says impatiently.

'It must have been the coma. The cover story we implanted has replaced his actual identity.'

The Russian snaps his fingers in my face.

'Eight!'

He stuffs his cigar in his mouth, looking me over proudly.

'What if I told you,' he resumes after a minute in a tone of greedy jubilation, 'that you're a fictional character?'

I defend myself with the same sincerity I've had for three days, except that now it's credible: I'm controlling it.

'And do you know how I know?' he continues. 'Because the fiction was devised by me.'

'He crammed your head full of gardening books, Disney pamphlets, and the Yale directory. You get it now?'

'It's a little more complicated than that,' says the conditioner. 'I programmed your identity as Martin Harris, your biography, the foundations of your character, and a file of botanical knowledge that you could dip into when you needed to be convincing.'

'Steven Lutz – ever heard of him?'

I shake my head mechanically, with no other reaction.

'That's you.'

My dumbfounded silence is met with a gesture of impatience.

'What really amazes me,' continues Netzky, searching in my eyes, 'is all the things your mind constructed from my basic outline. The quantity of memories you invented all by yourself. When Sabrina told me . . .'

'That's Liz, your wife,' explains Ralph. 'Sabrina Wells, actually, your partner on every contract for the past five years. Still nothing?'

I remain speechless, looking frozen, incredulous. The scar on her forehead was from the shattering eyeglasses, on October second, when I blew away the head of Senator Jackson from the hotel window overlooking the ticker-tape of the national debt. Why did my unconscious mask that incident so strongly?

'. . . when Sabrina told me what you said in the subway,' Netzky resumes, 'the intimate details I never programmed, entire scenes you described from a married life that never existed, I was amazed. Amazed by how the brain can elaborate a whole, logical world around a few bits of planted information.'

'Does that refresh your memory?' grumbles Ralph.

I shake my head again, as if the shock left me unable to utter a sound.

'I'll give you a hint, pal: you're part of Section 15.'

I repeat the number with my brows furrowed. My handler turns an icy face toward the Russian, who continues talking with increasing elation.

'Only once before have I seen things go so far . . . At the university in Leningrad, I hypnotized completely average art students into thinking they were Michelangelo. While under a trance, they drew in his style, but I discovered that the creative potential they developed continued to grow when they were back in their normal state. The result was, they become more and more talented, but in their own styles.'

'What *is* that – Section 15?'

'It's your family, Steve. A secret service so secret

that even the president doesn't know about it. For his own safety, of course. So he can't be implicated in our dirty work. Some joke, huh? You're not laughing. Obviously, you can't appreciate the irony . . .'

I don't see what's so new about it; he would hardly be the first head of state assassinated by his own security forces. This time they'll accuse the anti-American fanatics crawling all over France, just like they blamed the murder of Senator Jackson on the Mafia.

'That means, Steven,' the Russian continues, 'that the ability and world vision that these students had acquired, under the hypnotic influence of an artistic genius, leached into their own personalities, even when they were out of the trance! And that is exactly what has happened to you, but at a level I never would have expected . . .'

'Who gives a rat's ass?' Ralph interrupts.

'Maybe *you* should. I'm not just manufacturing cover stories for your killing machines – I'm giving people the possibility to completely modify their internal structure!'

'Go get some coffee, Netzky.'

The doctor replies that he isn't thirsty, that he

wants to understand how a few grafted memories, with no other external suggestion, were able to fabricate an autonomous virtual being and how – plop! he falls face forward, a hole in his skull.

'Intellectuals can be such a royal pain in the ass. What we need here, Steven, is not to understand the situation but to clean up a mess.'

I start trembling nervously, as convincingly as I can, while he announces the plan: the house will burn along with our corpses, Pascal will take care of my taxi girlfriend, and everything will be in place for tomorrow.

'Get ready to say your prayers, bud, assuming Martin Harris believes in God.'

I yelp out, '*why?*' over and over as he steadies his gun.

'If you only knew how lucky you've been, Steve . . . and how much trouble you've caused us since we pulled you from the mission.'

'What mission?'

He sighs, runs the silencer over the contours of my face.

'You fuck up your hand, we stash you here while we install another shooter in your place, you get spooked and take a hike, we catch up with you in the truck, run you into the river . . . First we think you're drowned, then safely in a coma, and then you show up at the apartment thinking you're just coming home. You bring out the neighbors, so we can't get rid of you on the spot, and *then* you go to the cops, you alert the embassy, you hire a detective to find out about you, you try every way you can to unmask your replacement . . . Of *course* he wasn't as convincing as you: Netzky only had six days with *him*.'

I ask him in a blank voice what the point of all this was.

'The point of what? Fabricating a botanist? That was your idea, when you found the apartment for rent online. Since its window looks out onto Elysée Palace, head office keeps a file on the occupants. We also had to find someone the owner would like, so we offered him a real stroke of luck: a tenant who could help prove his theories.'

I shake my head, looking dazed in my chair, broken by the collapse of what I believed was my life. I repeat over and over with dull obstinacy that

I'm Martin Harris. Ralph watches me, plainly disgusted.

'This hypnosis is a real son of a bitch,' he mutters, shoving the gun toward my mouth.

12

The sun rises behind the banana trees. The kid opens the umbrellas, drags mats onto the sand, arranges them, lies down to test them out. His sister passes by on a horse at the edge of the lagoon. He shouts at her to go gallop somewhere else; he's just finished raking the beach. Their mother opens the refreshment stand, a rosewood straw hut with a vetiver roof. I watch them from above. They're beginning to relax, to let their terror fade with the passing days, to assume this dream life that I've given them posthumously.

These days, Muriel Caradet is called Jeanne Grimm, a Swiss citizen who manages the Diamant Hotel on Mauritius Island, a quiet two-star at a remove from the palaces. Morgane is named Amandine, which she likes, but her brother thinks the name Cedric is even stupider than the one he used to have. With time, they're learning not to make mistakes, to accept their new faces. I, in any case, look much better. Not very expressive, perhaps; I miss the wrinkles around my eyes, the crow's feet that stretched toward my smile – but the sun will bring them back.

The flora here is amazing. Protected by the tangle of mangroves with aerial roots, a natural reserve flourishes, where exchanges between species fly in the face of all the laboratory theories. I'm making discoveries, re-examining all my received knowledge. All that erudition they put in my head – it had to go to some use. And it's my job to complete it. Of course I'm still an amateur; it's too late to start a career under another name with an artificial vocation. But I want to train Cedric. He is genuinely motivated, and it's a whole new thing to explore the Mauritian forest with him, to pass on to him everything they taught me and discover the rest together. He's already decided that he wants to be a botanist when he grows up. He'll carry on the torch.

I shimmy down the tree trunk, bring them a coconut. Cedric slices it in half with one chop of the machete and we share it under the umbrella in the soft morning air, in this illusion of a desert island before our customers disembark.

'Are you bringing him to school today?'

'Sure.'

Jeanne's smile brightens her face, which has been modified to my taste. She's pretending to be okay, but her personality no longer matches her appearance. By trying to protect her like this, I've taken away all her reference points, broken everything she'd built from the unfairness of fate and the pride of not owing anything to anyone. To make up for it, she spends twelve hours a day at the beck and call of the vacationers; exhaustion is her only mooring. How long will it be before we rediscover the chaotic magic of our night in Clichy? When will she be able to look the man I was in the face, chase away her doubts about my true nature, let our present erase my past? I wait. I love her in silence, wait for her to trust me again, and I watch over the family that I've built for myself.

She asks if I slept well. I say yes, hoping it will soon be true. Try as I might to clear my brain, every night I find myself going back, my dreams stirring up memories that no longer have anything to do with me – memories from a former existence that, in the light of day, I manage to stop believing in.

While Ralph Channing was sticking his gun in my mouth, I stabbed him. I set fire to the house as he had planned and rushed to the American embassy. When they heard the reason for my visit, they brought me straight up to the military attaché's office. I demanded to see the First Secretary, the legal department, to get on the hotline so I could negotiate directly with the CIA. Before giving the slightest bit of information about the planned assassination, I demanded to be put under witness protection. R-37, confidential: official death, plastic surgery, and new identity. The only arrangement that really works. I know from experience – I owe it the only two failed contracts of my career. I explained that, if they ever eliminated me, I had taken steps to make sure the plot would be revealed to the press. They have no way of knowing if I'm bluffing or not. They don't even know if I know who was behind the plot. I can guess, but I don't really care. The only truth I care about these days is the truth of our false ID papers.

The rest of it I learned like everyone else, from the news reports. On Friday night, a gas leak caused two deaths on Rue de Duras. Saturday morning, the President of the United States lunched at Elysée with his French counterpart. On the front steps, as they were shaking hands for the press, an explosion caused general panic. The security services immediately rounded up the group of photographers, but it was just a false alarm. The Dallas technique: an extra precaution to cover my replacement. While he had his target in his sights, the device Sabrina had planted in the camera would have made them think the fatal bullet came from a photographer. The time the police spent neutralizing him would have given the two of them a chance to clear out of the apartment before the area was cordoned off.

Since they couldn't hold him for an exploding flash bulb, the photographer was released two days later. The official version is that he died with us at the bottom of a ravine in the Val-de-Marne. At least he left some real human remains in the charred wreckage of the mini-van.

All that seems very far away now, with no connection to me. As the weeks go by, the in-dividuals who populated my former life have become more and more abstract. Much less real than the gardener father created out of a few hypnotic suggestions. The father who had taken form in my coma to tell me, *You'll have a second existence. Only you can decide what to do with it.* The voice of the unconscious, the refusal of the life I lived and that I couldn't get out of.

Steven Lutz is fading away. The persona of Martin Harris, and the feelings associated with his identity have grown over him, like ivy covering a dead tree. What remains of the man I was for forty-two years? That orphan of the Vietnam War, the precise and emotionless loner, the killing machine trained at West Point, broken in at Grenada, Palestine, Kuwait, refined at the training camp in Nevada, kept in reserve under cover of a real-estate agent in San Francisco; the man who spoke six languages, who could blend into a crowd, drop a target from three hundred yards, and assume any identity under hypnosis? What part of him have I kept? His physical form, his cautious reflexes, and three regrets: his piano, his two-story library with a view of the Golden Gate, and his cat, which the neighbors must have taken in.

All the rest – the cold violence inculcated since childhood, recruitment into the army, the false camaraderie of the training camp, the indifference to death, the price of blood converted into rare books – has left only surface traces. My state of mind was the result of a conditioning from which hypnosis one day delivered me. Thanks to a personality graft that *took root*. Thanks to the mystery of a coma that transformed a database into a human being. The six days during which I really believed I was someone else triggered a process in my head, the consequences of which I'm still discovering.

I'm not sure I really believe in redemption, but I'm giving it my best. In any case, I refuse to believe in fate, churning up the past, or remorse. What matters is not the harm I've done but the good I can do. I'll give it the time it needs, but I have faith in the power of my will. I will become for good the man I thought I was.